in, Staton.

curse of the Romanovs /

D0405670

THE CURSE OF THE ROMANOVS

ALSO BY STATON RABIN

Betsy and the Emperor
Black Powder

Margaret K. McElderry Books

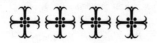

THE CURSE
OF THE
ROMANOVS

STATON RABIN

Margaret K. McElderry Books
New York   London   Toronto   Sydney

70176768

For my "troika" of great first readers:
Mark DeGasperi, Marian Natter, and Brandon Rabin.
And for my agents Donna Bagdasarian and Lynn
Pleshette, who give me that rarest of luxuries: the ability
to make a living doing something I enjoy.

With grateful appreciation to my editor, Karen Wojtyla,
a kind and supportive partner—and to Emma Dryden,
for her faith in me, and for getting a happy case of the
willies when I first told her this story.

Margaret K. McElderry Books
An imprint of Simon & Schuster Children's Publishing Division
1230 Avenue of the Americas, New York, New York 10020
This book is a work of fiction. Any references to historical events, real people,
or real locales are used fictitiously. Other names, characters, places, and
incidents are products of the author's imagination, and any resemblance to
actual events or locales or persons, living or dead, is entirely coincidental.
Copyright © 2007 by Staton Rabin
All rights reserved, including the right of reproduction in whole or in part in any form.
Book design by Michael McCartney
The text for this book is set in Minion.
Manufactured in the United States of America
10 9 8 7 6 5 4 3 2 1
Library of Congress Cataloging-in-Publication Data
Rabin, Staton.
The curse of the Romanovs / Staton Rabin.—1st ed.
p.   cm.
Summary: In 1916, teenage hemophiliac and heir to the Russian throne Alexei Romanov
escapes into the future to elude the murderous Rasputin, and meets his modern-day
cousin, fifteen-year-old Varda, who is working on a cure for hemophilia and who wants
to help change history by saving his family. Includes bibliographical references.
ISBN-13: 978-1-4169-0208-9 (hardcover)
ISBN-10: 1-4169-0208-2 (hardcover)
1. Aleksei Nikolaevich, Czarevitch, son of Nicholas II, Emperor of Russia, 1904-1918—
Juvenile fiction. [1. Aleksei Nikolaevich, Czarevitch, son of Nicholas II, Emperor of Russia,
1904-1918—Fiction. 2. Princes—Fiction. 3. Time travel—Fiction. 4. Hemophilia—Fiction.
5. Rasputin, Grigori Efimovich, ca. 1870-1916—Fiction. 6. Russia—History—Nicholas II,
1894-1917—Fiction.] I. Title.
PZ7.R1084Cur 2007 * [Fic]—dc22 * 2006014573

FIRST
EDITION

"Spasibo!" to Romanov historian and author Peter Kurth, and to Dr. Rex A. Wade (author, and professor of Russian history at George Mason University)—who both read this book in manuscript and were incredibly generous with their time, expertise, and support. Additional thanks to Neil Frick and Dr. Ann-Marie Nazzaro of the National Hemophilia Foundation, for their tremendous help in answering my questions.

© The State Hermitage Museum, St. Petersburg, Russia

Portrait of Tsarevich Alexei Nikolayevich
Mikhail Victorovich Rundaltsov

© The State Hermitage Museum, St. Petersburg, Russia

Portrait of Grigory Rasputin
Elena Nikandrovna Klokacheva

Gilliard—

The people of the future must learn the truth. The fate of Mother Russia and the world depends on it! Give this book to your children, and they to theirs. In December 2010 they must deliver it to an American girl, Varda Ethel Rosenberg, living in New York. She will know what to do.

I must go, my friend, spasibo. May God grant us peace in this unbearable and fearful hour!

Alexei

2:03 am 17 July 1918
Ekaterinburg, Russia

† † †

TSAR OF THE LAND

of Russia, if you hear the sound of the bell which will tell you that Grigory has been killed, you must know this: if it was your relations who have wrought my death, then no one of your family, that is to say, none of your children or relations, will remain alive for more than two years. They will be killed by the Russian people."

—*Grigory Rasputin, 1916*

"When I shall die, put up a small stone monument in the park to me."

—*Tsarevich Alexei Nikolaevich Romanov*

CHAPTER ONE

Spala, Poland, 1912
(Four years ago)

"MAMA! MAMA!—
it hurts! Please, God! Mama, come kill me!"

Three hundred years of my dead Romanov relatives crowded around my bedside, staring into my
bloodless pale face, wagging their ghostly heads with
concern. Great-grandpa Alexander—missing a leg
from the assassin's bomb—held out his bloody arms
to me in welcome. Peter the Great beckoned slowly,
slowly, inviting me into the land of death. There was
Ivan the Terrible, a pointy-toothed skull, grinning as
if he'd love my company—in hell. "Yes, Alyosha," he
hissed into my ear. "Wouldn't it be better for all to
just let go? Your poor mother's hair is turning gray.
Your father worries, your sisters, too. Just let go. It's
so easy. So easy . . ."

My eyes grew heavy. The icon lamps around my
bed flickered and faded. The light within my heart
was flickering, fading, too. Why, why didn't they call

Our Friend in time to save me? Why? Where are you, Father Grigory! So tired, so tired . . .

Just let go, let go. *Yes, Uncle Ivan, wouldn't it be better for all?* I rolled to one side and let out a last sigh.

A sudden lightning bolt of pain shot through my leg. Like marbles forced through my small veins. Yanking me, jolting me rudely back to the world of the living.

And then I screamed. A milkman's horse all the way in Tobolsk pricked up his ears at the sound.

Anxious clicking of shoes came down the hall. My mother burst through the door. The whites of her eyes red like borscht. Eyes staring at me in horror, ringed by the black of a thousand sleepness nights.

"God forgive me, baby!" she said, stuffing rags the color of snow into my mouth, muffling my screams.

You may think my mother cruel. But she was only protecting me. I shall explain. This will take time. I am not the author Chekhov, paid fifteen kopecks per line! You will have patience because I command it.

I was born in 1904, and on my *nynok*‡ the fate of Mother Russia was written. At six weeks of age I bled at the spot where I had once been joined to my mother. I bled, and I didn't stop bleeding. Dr. Botkin was called. He peered at my *nynok* over his pince-nez, as though examining a strange new purple fruit.

‡ *I have just asked my English tutor the word for "nynok." He says "belly button"! I am writing this book in English in case it falls into the hands of spies.*

"It's the same thing that killed my dear Frittie, isn't it?" my mama must have said, her skin turning gray like ashes from the fireplace. "The bleeding disease."

Frittie was her brother, who got hemophilia from my Grandma Alice. Who got it from her mother, Queen Victoria of England.

"I have not seen this myself before. But . . . yes, I'm afraid so. It can only be hemophilia," the doctor said.

And it was at that moment that I became my family's biggest secret.

What a difference from the day I was born!

Not every boy is greeted into this world by the firing of 301 guns and a whole country's rejoicing. And not every boy is given his own army regiment to command the moment he pops out of the womb. But not every boy is Tsarevich Alexei Nikolaevich Romanov, the future tsar of all the Russias, my family's precious Fabergé jewel, born after my sisters: four useless lumps of coal we call Olga, Tatiana, Mashka, and Anastasia.

How my mama tried to have a boy!

First they visited Mitka the Fool—babbling, in rags, naked. Mama's belly was already round. Mitka gave her a potion, made from special mushrooms that make the eyes see angels' halos. Mumble, mumble.

"What did he say?" Mama whispered to Papa.

"I think he said, 'You'll have a boy.'"

"Lovey—Lovey, you really think so?" She often calls him "Lovey."

"It's hard to say. . . ."

But Mama had another girl.

Next there was the witch, Daria Osipova. She writhed on the floor as if she had ants in her drawers. She gave Mama another potion: ramson, thorn apple, witch's grass. Mama drank, holding her nose. The room spun round in bright colors.

"Now swim in the river during a storm," Osipova advised. "When the pocked golden moon is rising. That is certain to make a boy."

Mama swam by the light of the moon, lightning storm raging. It's a wonder she didn't get herself electrocuted!

Instead Mama got herself . . . another girl.

Next, the weird Montenegrin princesses sent her Monsieur Philippe. Famous in France for his miracles. It was said Monsieur had special powers.

"Did you see me walking yesterday with Monsieur Philippe?" one of the Montenegrin princesses said to Mama.

"No, Militsa."

"Ah, but of course not! He made us both invisible!"

Mama was soon pregnant again. Joy of joys! But, alas, only a false pregnancy. And then another girl!

Philippe said it was Mama's fault. That she didn't have enough faith. Not enough faith! Mama, who prays day and night on her calloused knees for us? Mama, whose heart nearly broke when she gave up the German religion she was born with—so she could marry and embrace Papa's?

Monsieur Philippe said that someday another man of faith would come to help Mama in all ways. A holy man with deep penetrating eyes that see into your soul—more powerful, even, than he. Monsieur went back to France, and then he died. Or was invisible, forever, I suppose.

Mama was nearing the end of being able to make babies. She was tired. My parents had four girls; they were desperate. Who wouldn't be—with a palace full of chattering crows? Only boys can rule Russia. That is the law now—as it should be.

Then Father Ioann of Kronstadt told my parents of the miracle-worker, Serafim of Sarov, who'd died in 1833. Mama got Serafim canonized. She and Papa went to Sarov in the summer of 1903 to pray to the new saint—for the future me.

When I was born, my papa and sisters danced the mazurka! How could they have known then what was to come—that my *diadkas*‡ would sometimes have to carry me like a baby, long after I was one no longer?

‡ *My sailor-nannies, Nagorny and Derevenko.*

"*Give me a bicycle.*"

"*You know you cannot.*"

"*Mama, I want to play tennis like my sisters.*"

"*You know you dare not play.*"

"*Why aren't I like everyone else!*"

CHAPTER TWO

"THAT DAY AT OUR HUNTING LODGE IN SPALA in 1912—when my mother stuffed rags into my mouth—she was not granting my wish to die. She was only smothering my screams. No one must hear me, she said. It is dangerous to be a Romanov. Especially these days. *"Remember what they did to Great-grandpa Alexander—and to Uncle Serge. No one outside the family must know the future tsar is ill."*

But my French tutor, Gilliard, knew. Mama says Papa knows everything. But Gilliard knows *almost* everything.

Here is an example of how much Gilliard knows (Gilliard says a writer who gives no examples is no better than a fool): It happened four years ago—several months after my crisis at Spala.

"Your Highness," Gilliard said to my father one evening. "May I speak freely?" Gilliard does not bow. He does not believe in bowing—even to me. We were at

Tsarskoye Selo, as always during the winter, ever since things got too dangerous for us in St. Petersburg. I sat on a stool near them on the balcony, my leg straight now and almost healed. I was pasting photographs of our elephant—a gift from King Chulalongkorn of Siam—into the album. But the special glue Papa had ordered from England kept sticking to my fingers.

My father nodded to Gilliard, then sighed.

"You may speak. Not about Rasputin again, I hope. You know that the tsarina—"

"No, not Father Grigory. It's about the boy."

Papa seemed relieved. Now they had my attention. I pretended not to be listening.

"Yes?"

"He jumps, and his sailor-nannies catch him. He reaches, but they do the reaching for him. Almost before the thought even crosses his mind! How can the boy learn to discipline himself if others do it for him?"

"You know his special needs. You know the dangers."

Gilliard scratched his pointy beard impatiently.

"Yes, yes, I know the dangers. A bump, the merest injury, can mean suffering, months abed. Even death! But even more dangerous is this: a boy who will someday rule one sixth of the globe who cannot rule even his own impulses! A boy who never has a playmate except his doctors' sons and his own sisters! He knows nothing of his people. He knows nothing of the world!"

"You are his tutor. It is your job to teach him."

"What Alexei must learn to be a great tsar is not found in books. Not even in Tolstoy."

"We are done with Tolstoy," I said, forgetting that they weren't supposed to know I was listening. "He is tiresome. Papa is reading Sherlock Holmes to us now."

My father and Gilliard exchanged a smile. But Papa's smile quickly faded.

"I am a plain, simple man. When my father died, I was less prepared to be tsar than Alexei is now. But I learned! He is bright, he too will learn. In good time."

I felt as tall as my elephant. My father rubbed the place on his head that gave him headaches. The spot where a Japanese policeman had once sliced him with a sword. Cousin George had saved him, knocking the blade away just in time with his cane.

"But you will speak to Her Majesty about it?"

Even I was surprised to hear Gilliard challenge my father so boldly.

Papa sighed again and glanced at me, as if looking for some sort of sign. I winked at him.

At last, he nodded at Gilliard. Just then Papa's face lit up in an angel's smile. And I knew that my mother must have walked into the room.

Only she could make him smile like that.

Once, Grandpa Sasha held up the collapsed roof of a dining car, when his imperial train crashed at Borki. Twenty-one people died, and Grandpa held up the train's ceiling all by himself. Long enough so that Papa and the rest of his family could crawl to safety. That's what later killed Grandpa so young, the doctors said. The strain of holding up that car broke his kidneys. Well, sometimes it seemed that being tsar of Russia was like trying to hold up the roof of a train. And, lately, the roof was always caving in, with one revolution behind us, and talk of another to come. But my mama's love gave my father the strength to hold up the roof. Like Atlas holding up the whole world.

Spala, 1912

"When I am dead, it will not hurt anymore, will it, Mama?"

"No, darling. Never again. But you must not think like that."

"Oh, my leg—my leg! Where is Father Grigory?"

"Hush! Please, baby, someone will hear you! Our Friend had to go away for a while. You know how the people are—jealous, suspicious of saints. But he is praying for you."

"Oh, Mama! It hurts!"

"I know, darling, I know. I would give my heart, my soul—anything to take away your pain. When I think that it was my blood—my blood!—that did this to you, I—"

"It's not your fault, Mama!"

"Alexei—baby, you must promise me something."

"Yes, Mama?"

"Always take care of your sisters. And your father."

"Take care of him? But Papa is strong!"

"Papa is a good man, yes. But he is too kind—too kind for this cruel world! You are strong. Take my hand. There, that is good—such a fine, strong boy. Promise me, Alexei!"

"I promise, Mama."

Mama said my hand felt like a burning stove to her touch. Blood had pooled where my leg meets my body, forming a fiery, infected lump. Papa, broken with grief, ordered a bulletin drawn up, announcing my death.

But a telegram changed all our lives forever that day in Spala. Yes, a telegram! Do you doubt the word of the tsarevich?

"It is from Our Friend," my mother said, brow furrowing, reading it to herself. "In Siberia."

"Father Grigory...," I murmured gratefully through fevered lips as dry as buckwheat groats. "I knew he would! What does he say?"

"'God has seen your tears and heard your prayers. Do not grieve. The Little One will not die. Do not allow the doctors to bother him too much.'"

The wrinkle in my mother's brow flattened out. Like one of her chambermaids smoothing a sheet. By the next morning, my fever broke. I was on the way to being well again, though it would take a long time. And from that moment on, Mama needed Our Friend. Believing in him as she believed in the Holy Mother. We knew that Father Grigory was the man of God that Monsieur Philippe had promised would someday come help Mama and make us all safe again. With deep blue eyes that could penetrate deeply into our souls. From that moment on, my *sudba* and Father Grigory's—yes, his destiny, ours, and Mother Russia's—were all written in the same blood.

CHAPTER THREE

Tsarskoye Selo
December 1916 (now)

NEXT SUMMER I WILL BE THIRTEEN—
about the same age Papa was when he saw his
grandpa Alexander blown to little bits by an assassin
in St. Petersburg. Grandpa's belly was torn open, his
legs were crushed. The grenade exploded with such
force that broken pieces of his gold wedding band
were imbedded in his hand. This is why Papa's eyes
look like they have seen too much.

They carried what was left of Grandpa from the
street to his Winter Palace. Leaving a trail of red
on the white marble stairs. Grandpa was still alive.
The doctors plugged him with rags to try to stop
the bleeding, but they knew it was hopeless. If only
Father Grigory had known us then—he could have
saved him!

The doctors rung out the bloody rags in water
basins brought by the servants. People dipped their
hands in the red water—like holy water.

† † †

"Gilliard, is my family cursed?"

"What nonsense! Where do you get such silly ideas?"

"Gleb‡ told me. He said Mama came to Russia walk-ing behind Grandpa Sasha's coffin, and brings us bad luck. And on the day Mama ‡Gleb is one of Dr. Botkin's sons. *and Papa were crowned, everyone rushed in for free souvenir mugs. A thousand peasants got crushed to death. Like ants!"*

"And what did you say when Gleb told you this?"

"Nothing. I punched him."

"Alexei! You are older than Gleb, bigger than he is. What would your mother say?"

"I know what Papa would say. He would say, 'Good for you!'"

After the war with Japan and our revolution in 1905—and Uncle Serge getting blown up—we Romanovs mostly stuck close to home. Safe in our little nest at Tsarskoye Selo, in the Alexander Palace. Only one hundred rooms—we live like peasants! We are rarely seen out in public. They say we Russians are too serious. Da, maybe so! But even Romanovs know how to play. When I am sick in bed, the girls take turns clowning in my room. "Who am I now, who am I now?" Anastasia says, making a face—imitating one of the servants dropping a tray when they tripped him, or Dr. Botkin's worried squint. Botkin wears so much cologne that my sisters can find him anywhere in the palace, just by running down hallways sniffing the air!

When Father Grigory fixes me up again, the Romanovs build snow mountains—even Papa! After morning lessons with my tutors of French, English, and Russian (Gilliard, Gibbes, and Petrov), my sisters skate while I play Winged-S biplane—"zoom, zoom!"—my *diadkas* watching me like hawks in case I take a spill. We make photographs of each other, then of ourselves in the mirror, and play Nain Jaune. At night we read ghost stories, or howl at Charlie Chaplin in two-reelers projected onto a white sheet. Or the girls act in plays. Fat Mashka, our faithful little "bow-wow," always plays the boy—in a tricorne hat!

And sometimes under cover of darkness we all sneak out to the Mariinsky Theatre in St. Petersburg. Once, we even got to see Nijinsky and Pavlova, the greatest ballet dancers in the world. That night I sat overlooking the balcony railing, with the Big Pair to one side of me, the Little Pair‡ on the other. The Imperial Guard made Papa sit in the darkness behind us. To make him a harder target for assassins. Mama had sciatica again and stayed home, embroidering shirts for Father Grigory.

‡*Big Pair: my eldest sisters, Olga and Tatiana. Little Pair: the younger ones, Mashka (our nickname for Marie) and Anastasia.*

On the ride over to the Mariinsky, I was alone with Papa in one carriage. We do not often get to be alone! My sisters rode together in the carriage that followed.

"Did you remember to kiss your Mama good-bye?"

"Yes, Papa. But I think I am getting too old for it."

"You see me kiss Grandma Minnie. Yes, every time I go away. Never too old! Always remember." He looked out the carriage window at the streets of St. Petersburg as dark shadows fell across the steps of the Winter Palace, and he sighed. "You never know what God has in store. . . . Each kiss may be the last."

"Yes, Papa."

He turned back to face me. Now staring intently, with moist eyes as clear and blue as the Neva.

"I will not be here forever. You must always take care of your sisters, Alexei. And your mama. She is not strong. She wants everyone to think she is! Your mama has many crosses to bear."

"I know, Papa." One of those crosses was me.

He looked down at his hands—at his golden wedding ring.

"Alix was only twelve when I saw her for the first time at Peterhof. She was visiting Russia for Aunt Ella's wedding to Uncle Serge. And I knew right then—yes, I knew! 'I'm Nicky,' I said, trembling like the schoolboy I was. 'I'm Sunny,' she said—that was her nickname. And I felt the touch of her soft hand like rose petals in mine. 'Yes, I know,' I replied, my wits deserting me. The people say she doesn't smile—but they don't know Alix like we do. It is only because she is shy! Your mama smiled that first day for me. I asked Grandma Minnie for a diamond brooch, to give to Alix. We danced that night at the children's ball. Alix stabbed the pin into my hand!"

"Heavens! On purpose? Why would Mama do that?"

"Oh, I was being much too forward. Who could blame her? But I was in love!"

"And was Mama in love too?"

"We carved our names together into the window glass at Peterhof. The very week we met. I will show you next time we visit—it's still there."

I whispered to my sister Anastasia as a girl in a tutu and pink ballet slippers spun circles onto the stage of the Mariinsky. "It's Pavlova! Beautiful—like the Snow Maiden! Look! She has silver fairy dust in her hair!"

My sister cocked her head at me, raising an eyebrow—as always when she is ready for mischief.

"The apple doesn't fall far from the tree! Papa had an affair with a ballerina, you know."

"What?"

"It's true! Before he married Mama, of course. Grandma Minnie and Grandpa Sasha pushed the ballerina on him. They didn't want Papa to marry Mama, but he never gave up. The dancer's name was Mathilde Kschessinska."

"Liar!"

She shrugged, turning away, and looked back toward the stage. "Ask Olga or Mashka if you don't believe me." She knew that Tatiana was Mama's favorite and too "good" to gossip.

"Shhh!" My other sisters leaned over, hissing at us like angry geese. We got angry glances too from the St. Petersburg society ladies, staring at us over their lorgnettes.

Then Nijinsky made his entrance. His tights were very tight—you could see everything, almost! All the ladies went "Ahhhhhhh!"—and even a few men! He was half man, half animal—all genius. I had to pry the opera glasses away from Anastasia to steal a better look.

Then Nijinsky leaped. The dancer rose straight up, up from the stage—two meters, three, four—more! Then he hung absolutely motionless at the peak. Impossible! Hundreds held their breath. Nijinsky stayed suspended in the air like mountain mist. Frozen in time. Then at last we exhaled as he sailed back down slowly to earth, like a leaf on an autumn breeze.

If only I could fly like Nijinsky! No one to stop him, or tell him *nyet*. No nervous *diadkas* to catch him if he falls.

After the ballet, Papa took us to meet Nijinsky backstage. The dancer was still in his theater makeup, so his eyes were sharply outlined in black, his skin was painted bronze, and his cheeks were rosy. Long, furry-pointy faun's ears sprouted from the sides of his head. He was just buttoning his shirt over his bare chest as we walked in. My sisters stared at the dancer, like a pack of she-wolves who hadn't had dinner in months. He winked at them, then turned to me.

"Ah, you must be Tsarevich!" Nijinsky said in his funny Polish-Ukrainian accent, bowing. Then he reached to shake the hand I held out to him. "So tall and strong, already—grrrrr, what a grip!" Nijinsky held his arm limply, pretending I'd broken it, to amuse me. "Maybe you become dancer like the great Nijinsky, yes? Come tour Paris with Mr. Diaghilev's Ballets Russes and me—and kiss French girls. Shall I teach you dance?"

"Yes, yes!"—how I longed to say. "Let me fly with you! We'll even take Anastasia, if she is good. Any-where—anywhere! We shall fly together like Peter Pan, Michael, and Wendy!"

But I could not tell Nijinsky the truth. No flying for me.

Ashamed, I looked down at my feet and said nothing.

"So very kind of you, Mr. Nijinsky," my father jumped in. "But you see, I'm afraid my son Alexei is very busy studying to be tsar."

"Ah, too bad, Your Majesty. The boy would have made fine dancer, no? But of course, I understand. He will make even better tsar! Please, call me Vaslav. Both of you."

Papa let me hand a bouquet of flowers to Pavlova. She smelled of baby's powder, pancake makeup—and nicely musky like sweat. But I couldn't stop dreaming of flying with Nijinsky.

Not long after that, even the thought of walking again would seem like a hopeless dream.

CHAPTER FOUR

IT HAPPENED AT TSARSKOYE SELO, just a few weeks later.

I awoke in the half-light of morning, exhausted from pain. Dr. Botkin's mud-bath treatments had done nothing for me. I'd spent a hard night. Through the first light of morning I could just make out in the hallway the dark form of a man wearing a sable overcoat. He was leaving the room of the children's nurse, Maria Vishnyakova, closing the door quietly behind him. When the man turned back, I saw a flash of gold—from a heavy gold cross, which I recognized as a gift from my mother. Father Grigory! Maria, still in her nightdress, ran out after him into the hallway. She clutched at his back, sinking slowly to her knees. Her shoulders shook with her sobs.

"Shhhh! Get up, woman! It is no sin," Father Grigory said in his rough but soothing voice. "Not when it is a holy act that cleanses the spirit." He pulled Maria to her feet.

Then I recognized my mother's footsteps—not as rapid as they'd been before her leg pain from sciatica. She was coming around the bend in the hall. Father Grigory pressed a guiding hand on Maria's shoulder, and she quickly disappeared back into her room.

"My darling!" Mama said, approaching, kissing Father Grigory's hands. "Thank God you have come!"

"How is the boy?"

"Worse every minute! He bumped his hip getting out of the bathtub—for days, Alexei hid this from me! His fever was over one hundred and four last night. And the pain! Grigory, Grigory, he begged me to take his life again! Can you imagine that for a mother to hear? I stayed with him, praying to the Holy Mother till he cried himself to sleep." She glanced nervously from side to side. "Did anyone see you come in?"

"No one."

"Good." She led him into my room. I quickly shut my eyes and pretended to be sleeping.

I smelled Father Grigory's hand—smoke, leather, ladies' perfume—before I felt its familiar gentle roughness touch my forehead.

"Peace, Alyosha," he said, whispering my nickname in his coarse Siberian accent, as comforting to me as a Tchaikovsky serenade. "Father Grigory is here." I smelled vodka on his breath.

He must have taken off his coat, because I felt a silk sleeve brush my cheek.

"Still has high fever," Grigory said to my mother. "Go—leave us now. Do not worry your head anymore."

My mother, obedient, left us.

Father Grigory gave me a couple of love-taps on the cheek.

"Hah! You think you fool Father Grigory?" he said after my mother had left the room. "How long you listen? You are awake like the sparrows in May! Open them."

I opened one eye, squinting in the now-bright morning light streaming through my window.

"Go on. Both!"

I opened my other eye.

"I wasn't listening, I just did not want to worry Mama. How did you know I was awake?"

He smiled at me. "Father Grigory sees past, he sees future, sees even things he doesn't want to know. How do you feel?"

"I can't bend my leg! It's all twisted up like—"

"Bah! Never mind. Father Grigory fix. Look at me, Alexei."

I looked up at his face and found his eyes. Or, rather, they found me.

I never wanted to look into Father Grigory's eyes, but could never stop myself. They belonged to a creature of the forest, not one who walks on two feet. Some found their souls in those clear, steel blue eyes, others lost theirs. Most saw the fires of hell in them, but a few, like my mama, saw only heaven. Only Father Grigory's eyes could tame my bleeding. But people said they made women wild—and drove brave men mad. He took my hand.

As he mumbled a prayer, Father Grigory's face turned yellow and waxy like a corpse. Suddenly he was struck by invisible lightning—trembling, moaning. Vibrating energy shot up one arm, down the other—right to my hand where it joined his. I was holding a bare electrical wire with my feet in water. I couldn't let go! I screamed from a hundred fathoms deep inside my soul, too deep for anyone to hear me. Father Grigory went rigid, his eyes rolled back in his head. Then he slumped over my bed—a rag doll.

Slowly he raised himself, like Lazarus rising from the dead.

"It is done," he said, and made the sign of the cross.

And soon I could walk again—at least till next time.

But even Father Grigory's great and mysterious power had its limits. He could heal me, but not cure me. He could stop my bleeding, but not bombs or bullets. And, next to my illness, these were what my mother feared the most.

CHAPTER FIVE

GILLIARD ALWAYS WRITES IN RED PENCIL

on my papers: "Alexei, how many times must I tell you? Relate events in their proper order! First this happened, second that, third—something else."

But I say that this is my life, I shall tell it in any order I please! Gilliard scowls when I say this and scolds me. But the Tsarevich does not follow rules; he makes them.

So now I will tell you about something important that happened to me a few years ago.

It was 1913—our family's three-hundredth anniversary. Three hundred years since Michael, the first Romanov, had taken the Russian throne.

"We must let the people see us, my dear," Papa said to Mama. "The *mouzhiks*, who work hard and till the soil, they love their tsar like a child its mother! It is only a few troublemakers. Only a few bad apples who try to make the people discontented."

"It only takes one to take your life," Mama said grimly.

"I was born on the day of the long-suffering Job, and am prepared to meet my destiny."

Papa rode out in front of the big anniversary procession in Moscow, down the street leading to the gates of the Kremlin. No Cossack regiment to guard him with their rifles and sabers. No carriage to shield him. Just Papa alone on his horse—slowly riding forward, sitting up straight as a samovar in the saddle, while the people on both sides of the Prospekt cheered him and sang, "God save the tsar!" Yes, cheering and singing! We rode behind in our carriages. I was never so proud of Papa as I was that day.

How different this was from the days of the 1905 revolution, when the people sang:

> Nicholas, tsar, praise be to you!
> Our sovereign, devil's son too
> Merciless butcher, be drowned in blood
> Let all Romanovs meet death in the flood
> Like maggots will perish all of your kin
> You will also die because you have sinned
> Kept people in jails, many are dead
> Millions of others have no bread!

As for me, I was sick again during the time of our three-hundredth anniversary celebrations, and could not walk. My parents prayed to Saint Serafim that I would be well in time for the main ceremonies. But it was not to be.

"Has His Majesty ever noticed," Gilliard said to Papa, "that Alexei always seems to take ill just when he must appear in public?"

Nonsense! Gilliard reads too much philosophy!

Back in St. Petersburg, Nagorny carried me in his arms—into Kazan Cathedral behind my parents and sisters. The church candle flames bowed in a sudden gust of air as every head turned as one to look at us. Nagorny walked slowly—so terribly slowly!—down the aisle.

"Hurry up, tortoise!" I whispered in Nagorny's ear. But I knew his instructions from my parents were to not risk dropping me.

"Poor lamb . . ." The people's anxious whispers echoed off the church's stone walls like a Byzantine chant. Their stares at me—unbearable!

"Look, Anya—the tsarevich!"

"The heir! What's wrong with him?"

"What's wrong?"

"—touched the hem of his uniform! Yes, with this very hand!"

"He's an angel—"

How I wished again that I could fly away—and go anywhere, *anywhere* but here!

"—the spawn of the devil!"

"They say he's not well!"

"It's his heart—"

"—his spleen!"

"Rabies! A dog bit him!"

"—scarlet fever!"

"The boy is a cripple!"

"I sent him an icon from Kiev. It cost me fifty kopecks!"

"The tsarina never smiles—this is why!"

"I pray to the Holy Mother for him!"

"Bloody Nicholas and his cursed German witch! Only got what they deserve!"

"—what they deserve!"

"Dear God! What will become of Mother Russia?"

At last we sat down in our row. I could breathe again!

I spotted Father Grigory seated down in front. Raising my hand, I was going to wave to him. But Papa put his hand on my arm to stop me. We waited for the Te Deum to begin.

Then, suddenly, Mr. Rodzianko, the president of the Duma, strode over to Father Grigory.

"You are sitting in a Duma member's seat. Clear out at once, you vile heretic!"

Rasputin looked up at the man, as if calmly studying a fly that had landed on his picnic basket.

Mama instantly grabbed Papa's arm. I heard her whisper, "Nicky! Do something!" But Papa didn't move a muscle. He knew that the people did not like Our Friend and that the tsar must not be seen defending him in public.

"There is no place for you in this sacred house!" Rodzianko said, yanking Father Grigory up by the collar.

Father Grigory struggled free of Rodzianko's grip. Our Friend was as strong as a Siberian tiger, from all the hard labor he had done as a boy in Pokrovskoe.

"Oh, Lord, forgive him such sin!" Father Grigory said.

"Don't look," Papa whispered urgently into my ear. "Just stare straight ahead." I was dying to see, but I did as I was told. The next thing I heard was the sound of Father Grigory's patent leather boots stomping up the aisle. Then the heavy wooden door of Our Lady of Kazan slamming behind him.

I was up half that night, moaning with pain. Begging again for Death to come take me.

But it was not Death that came, but Father Grigory. The moment he walked into my room, my pain went away for a little while—like a bad schoolboy sent to sit in the corner.

Father Grigory shook the snow from his sable coat, and tossed it over a chair. Then he sat down next to me, and did all the strange and mysterious things he always did when I was ill—which never failed to calm my fever and tame my bleeding.

"You are so good to us!" I said to him moments later, when his work was done and he had stood up to leave. "Why do they hate you so?"

"Do not speak, Little One. You must save your strength. Like kopecks for a rainy day."

"But, *why*?"

He sat down on my bed again, and sighed.

"Until Grigory was twenty-eight, he live for pleasure. Grigory lived, as people say, 'in the world.' Then one night I sleep in room where there was icon of the Mother of God. And I wake up in middle of night and see icon is weeping. But I am not afraid. 'Why do you cry?' I ask. 'Grigory,' she says, 'I am weeping for the sins of mankind. Go, wander, and cleanse the people of their sins.' I give up everything, become *strannik*, wander thousands of versts. I have done what she ask."

"And for this the people hate you?"

He shrugged.

"Some people do not like to be reminded of sins they wish to forget."

"Cousin Felix says you drink vodka—and bathe with women!"

"The saints did also! What is strength without temptation? But, da, Alexei, Grigory is sinner."

"Are my parents sinners?"

"They are good, they are holy. But, da—as all. They are sinners too."

"Surely not Mama!"

He gently put his hand on my chest and pressed me back down against my fluffy pillows. He pulled the covers up under my chin.

"No more talk now, Alyosha—rest. You just listen, eh?" He took my small, pale hand in his rough peasant's one. "What would tsarevich do if he could do anything?"

I opened my mouth to speak, but he put his fingers on my lips.

"Shush! No talk. Just tell me with mind."

I pictured Nijinsky—dancing. And airplanes.

Father Grigory shut his eyes and seemed to be thinking very hard. Then he opened his eyes.

"Ah! Very good choice. So Alexei wants to fly, eh? Father Grigory will teach."

"You know how to *fly*?"

"Shhhh. Better than fly." He unfastened an emerald and silver pin from his shirt. The pin had my mother's initials carved on it, and had been a secret gift from her. With a quick, jerky motion Father Grigory stabbed the pin into his thumb. I gasped, grabbing his hand.

"Father!"

A dark ruby glob glistened on the tip of his thumb like a bead on a Fabergé egg. He smiled, examining the bead curiously as if he'd never seen blood before.

"It is but a drop, Little One. But it contains whole universe! Open your mouth. Open it!"

I obeyed. He touched the drop of blood to my tongue, like giving Holy Communion.

"Taste the future, taste the past. Blood is river of

time, joining you to Mama and Papa, yes. But also to Romanovs yet unborn! Using mind, Alexei can travel to future to see them."

I stared at him, raising an eyebrow.

"You doubt word of Grigory? I have done this myself, with own family. Traveling down blood-river of time. I have seen my son's great-great-grandson in America, who is not yet born till almost one hundred years. I have seen this—da!—with own eyes! You can 'fly' also this way, Alyoshenka. If you only believe."

I shook my head. Father Grigory tilted my chin up so that my eyes met his.

"Using power of mind, Alexei can escape anytime. When boy bleeds, imagine blood-river carry him to another place, future time. Go where all is peaceful, no more pain. See future relatives. But always remember: Tsarevich must travel only with mind, *not with body*. Travel forward with body, Alexei will never return."

He patted me on the cheek.

"Now. We give try, da? Close eyes and breathe deep."

I shut my eyes.

"That's right . . . slowly. See only with mind. Never fear blood—is life force that powers mind. Count to yourself. Count to *desyat*."

"*Odin, dva, tri—*"

"To yourself!"

"Sorry."

"Shhh! Begin again."

I counted in my head.

"That's right, Alyosha. Very good. Breathe in, breathe out. *Tri, chetyre, pyat* . . . Sleep. . . . Falling deeper as you count. *Shest, sem* . . . deeper and deeper . . . *vosem, devyat.* . . . Falling, falling—into the deepest, softest feather pillow. *Desyat.* Now, fully asleep. Good. You swim now in river of time. River is bright red, like blood rushing through vein. Swept along by current, you swim faster and faster. Feel it now—warm river of time against skin."

I quivered.

"Repeat after me," Father Grigory said. "Mother of God . . ."

"Mother of God."

"Say, 'Blood of the tsar.'"

"Say Blood of the tsar."

"Just repeat phrase!"

"Blood of the tsar."

"I have no fear."

"I have no fear."

"Now take me far!"

"Take me far."

"Now. What does tsarevich see, where time river take him?"

"I see . . . I see a dark naked man with muscles. Holding the whole world up on his shoulders."

"Hmmm . . . what else?"

"Now I see . . . a big blue lake. With a little black

island floating in the middle. And a row of bare trees growing on one shore of the lake."

"Da?"

"The trees—they're moving! The whole row together, sweeping across the lake. Wait! It's not a lake. It's a big eye! Like a giant's eye. It's blinking! The row of trees—they're eyelashes!"

Just then a woman spoke.

"Another one of your games?"

It was my mother's voice. Father Grigory clapped his hands—once, twice, three times. I awoke very suddenly and opened my eyes. Mama had come into the room.

"Yes, Tsarina," Father Grigory said, tugging at his beard. "Alexei and I were playing 'let's pretend.' Shall you join us?" He stared at her a long time, and my mother's cheeks turned pink.

"I don't like the way he looks at me. As if he's seen me without my corset on!"

"Olga! Father Grigory would never do such a thing."

"It's true, Tatiana. Last night, when I was putting on my nightdress. The door was open, just a crack. I swear by the Holy Mother—I caught him peeking at me from the hallway. Like—like some kind of—"

"Shhh! That's sacrilege! Alexei's in his room. He might hear you!"

"You think the boy doesn't know? Don't be a fool. Alexei's ill, he's not stupid. He knows everything."

"She's right, you know. I've caught Father Grigory looking at me, too. When I was coming out of the bathtub, and had only a towel on. Truth be told, I kind of enjoyed it."

"Me too."

"Anastasia! Mashka! I'm going to tell Mama on you!"

The girls' governess, Madame Tiutcheva, complained to Mama about Father Grigory. She said he was staring at them in their nighties. And even though Mama was angry at her for doubting our man of God, from that moment on he was no longer allowed near my sisters' rooms.

One day when my *diadka* Nagorny wasn't looking, I looked through his knapsack, and found cruel newspaper articles about Father Grigory. They said that Rasputin made Mama and Papa dance to his tune, like puppets on a string. That he drank. And Anastasia told me she'd heard soldiers laughing at ugly cartoons, showing Father Grigory with women. Mama said it was all vicious gossip. The saints, they kissed everyone too, she said. Mama was deaf to any complaints about him.

Once, while I was throwing a ball to my dog Joy outside Papa's working study, Metropolitan Anthony went in to see Papa about Father Grigory. I heard Father Anthony say that Rasputin must go.

"The Church has no right to interfere in my family's private business," Papa replied.

"No, sire," Father Anthony said. "This is not merely

a family affair, but the affair of all Russia. The tsarevich is not only your son but our future sovereign, and belongs to all Russia."

Not long after that, the Metropolitan suddenly dropped dead. I never found out why or how.

Then Father Iliodor told Papa that he had heard Father Grigory boast of taking advantage of a nun. Father Iliodor and Bishop Hermogen beat Our Friend with a wooden cross, and made him promise not to do it again.

Even the prime minister complained to Papa about Rasputin. The line of people waiting to tell tales about Our Friend grew longer. But I knew they were only jealous of Father Grigory's friendship with us. I did not believe their terrible lies.

Still, the voices against Our Friend got so loud that even Papa agreed we had to do something. If only to keep the people happy. So from time to time, he sent Father Grigory away. Mama was afraid of what would happen to us without him. But Papa was her tsar, and she had to obey him like anyone else. So for a few months Father Grigory traveled in the Holy Land. And sometimes Papa sent Father Grigory home to Siberia—to his wife Praskovia and his sons and daughters.

Luckily for me, my health stayed good while Our Friend was away. But whenever I was bored or lonely, I remembered the mysterious place waiting for me at the end of the river of time—the strange and wonderful land that he had taught me how to visit with my mind. I'd shut my eyes, count from *odin* to *desyat*, then imagine myself swimming—*nyet*, almost flying!—down a fast-moving red river of blood. But I also remembered Our Friend's warning, which frightened me. So I would always stop myself before my imagination carried me too far.

Still, I could not stop wondering about the strange pictures he had painted in my mind. What did they mean? The man holding up the world. Could that be Papa—or Grandpa Sasha holding up the roof of the train in Borki? And what about the big blue eye, the eye of a giant? A strange dream. Or *was* it a dream?

CHAPTER SIX

WE SPENT THE SPRING

and summer of 1914 as we did every year: staying at
golden Peterhof palace, then sailing the emerald sea
around the Finnish skerries in our yacht, *Standart*.
Dropping anchor here and there to have picnics
ashore. Mama had the rheumatism and was happy
to stay on the boat and do her sewing. Gilliard spent
more time reading scandalous French novels than
scolding me. The girls spent their lazy days flirting
with the young officers of the guard. Dancing with
them to the *Standart*'s balalaika orchestra, then going
to the ship's chapel to pray for forgiveness at having
too much pleasure. How convenient!

Papa played at burying me in the soft yellow
sand. The corners of my father's eyes crinkled like
Carpathian walnut shells when he smiled. For once
he did not seem to be holding up the whole world on
his shoulders.

But as we Russians say, beware the quiet dog or still water. Just four days into our peaceful summer voyage, Papa got a telegram. It said that Archduke Ferdinand and his wife had been murdered in Bosnia.

"Ferdinand? Who is he, Gilliard?"

"This is bad news for Russia, Alexei, very bad. Franz Ferdinand was to inherit the throne of Austria. Politics were at a delicate stage already. And now this murder— the last thing we needed! All the countries of Europe will blame one another for his death. I fear that Russia— and much of the world—may get pulled into it."

The next day, we got news from Siberia that was even worse. Papa hid the telegram from Mama, so he could break the news to her gently. But Mama fainted anyway.

"The knife missed his vital organs. The Lord was with him," Papa told her after Dr. Botkin's smelling salts woke her up. "And with the Lord's help, he will recover."

"Dear God! My poor Grigory!" Mama wailed. "We must all pray for him!"

Father Grigory had been stabbed in the stomach by a woman. When she plunged in the knife, she shouted, "I have killed the Antichrist!"

Our Friend recovered. Mama said it was a miracle, and proof that Father Grigory was a saint. But I think he must have healed himself, as he had so often healed me.

We returned to Peterhof, where Papa met with

Monsieur Poincaré, the president of the French Republic. For a while we didn't know which way the wind was blowing. But at last Gilliard's prediction about what would happen after the archduke was killed came true.

"The Duma was in every way worthy of the occasion," Papa reported to Mama after returning from his meeting in St. Petersburg. "It expressed the will of the nation, for the whole of Russia smarts under the insults heaped upon it by Germany. I have the greatest confidence in the future now. I have done everything in my power to avert this war, and I am ready to make any concessions consistent with our dignity and our national honor."

But one night, two weeks before my tenth birthday, Papa came to us while we were eating. We all dropped our forks at his words.

"We are at war with Germany."

Mama wept, and seeing our strong mother weep, my sisters did too. Germany was her land, her people. What would this mean for the country of Mama's birth? The Kaiser was our own Cousin Willy—who Papa said should be locked up in a madhouse. Mama and Father Grigory had been against the war, but Mama understood that Papa had had no choice. My father sat down at the table with us and sighed heavily. The world was on his shoulders again.

When Papa made the public announcement of war, thousands fell to their knees outside the Winter

Palace. The people sang his praises with the imperial hymn. Papa and Mama waved to the crowd from the balcony.

"You cannot imagine how glad I am that all the uncertainty is over," Papa said to Gilliard as they walked with me at Peterhof soon after, "for I have never been through so terrible a time as the days preceding the outbreak of war. I am sure that there will now be a national uprising in Russia like the great War of 1812."

By "uprising" Papa meant that he was sure the people would support us. And for a while he was right.

All of Russia praised the tsar. They joined hands together around Papa and the war. But toward Mama the people were not generous. Mama, Olga, and Tatiana took a course in nursing from the Red Cross. Mama set up a hospital, right at Tsarskoye Selo. She and the girls sewed up soldiers' wounds, prayed with them. And still the people said that Tsarina Alexandra—born Princess Alix of Hesse-Darmstadt—was the enemy. Even a German spy!

Didn't they know that Mama had really been raised by Queen Victoria—after her British mother Princess Alice had died? Mama thought herself more English than German. All her letters to Papa were in English, and she spoke to us in nothing else. Germany was her country of birth, this is so. But Mama was as true a

Russian as any of us when it came to her love for us and Papa—and whose side she was on in this war.

Our people hated anything German. So they started calling sauerkraut "liberty cabbage." And they even renamed Peter the Great's beautiful capital city "Petrograd," because they thought St. Petersburg sounded too "German"!

But soon Russia knew that Mama and Father Grigory had been right about the war. It came at a heavy cost. Within the first few months, we had already lost about a quarter of a million soldiers. Imagine! That's as if everyone in a large Russian city suddenly dropped dead all at once.

In 1904, the year I was born, we had been at war with Japan. Gilliard says we lost nearly our whole fleet at the Battle of Tsushima the next year. After that there were shortages of weapons and food. That war had ended badly for us. There were workers' strikes, and the Russian people revolted. Uncle Serge was murdered by revolutionaries. Grandma Minnie called it "the year of nightmares." Papa was forced to sign the October Manifesto and make our legislature, the Duma. I say "forced" because of what Olga told me. "Dread Uncle" Nikolasha took out a gun, put it to his own head, and said he'd shoot himself if Papa did not sign the constitution. Does that not sound to you like he was forced?

Papa dissolved the Duma but let it come back again. Things were quiet for a while. Mr. Stolypin, our prime minister, made reforms that let more peasants own land. And our soldiers had a great victory in Galicia. But then history seemed to repeat itself.

"The people are discontented, Alexei. Just like during our war with Japan. Our soldiers do not have enough weapons or clothing. Farmers are leaving their fields to fight in the war. Their families, wives and children left behind, are starving. And they are blaming your mama and papa for it."

"Gilliard, you know that is not so. I could have Papa arrest you for saying so!"

"Yes, I know you could. I will say it in a whisper. But I will say it, just the same, because the future tsar of all the Russias needs to know the truth about his people. And no one else will tell you."

In the fall of 1915, during the second year of the war, Mama let me visit Papa at Stavka‡ in Mogilev. ‡*Military headquarters* She cried enough tears to fill the Baltic when she and my sisters said good-bye to me at the train station.

"Don't wipe out the whole German army by your-self," Anastasia teased. "You must leave something for Papa and our soldiers to do."

"Here's some piroshki," my sister Olga said, handing a warm bag to me. "I made them myself. I heard the food is terrible at headquarters."

"Mashka has gotten fat on them!" Anastasia said, and Mashka gave her a sharp push that nearly knocked her off the train platform.

"Don't worry," Tatiana said. "We'll take good care of Joy." I handed my little spaniel over to her waiting arms. My dog looked at me with sad eyes, as if he knew I would not be back for a while.

"Baby, you look so grown up in your uniform!" Mama said, giving me one last hug like she'd never let go. "Take care not to fall or bump yourself. And remember what I said. Take good care of Papa."

"Yes, I will. Mama, please don't call me 'baby' anymore," I whispered.

She did not want me to go. But she knew Papa was lonely in Mogilev without us. Gilliard went with me, to keep up our lessons. He promised to write Mama every day to tell her how I was.

I slept on an iron camp bed in Papa's room at Stavka. There was hardly enough room to turn around, and no army of servants to attend me. The food tasted like pig slop. We lived like peasants. But I was never so happy.

Still, there was one thing I was *not* happy about.

"Papa, I want to fight for Russia like the rest of our soldiers!"

"You are much too young, Alexei. And besides, you must stay safe. Your country needs you to be tsar one day."

"They will think I'm a coward if I don't fight! Father Grigory's son is a soldier! How can we ask the people to send their sons if you won't send yours?"

Papa did not answer me.

"Maybe I will die young anyway."

"Alexei! Who told you that?"

"Nobody. I heard Dr. Botkin and Dr. Derevenko‡ talking about me."

‡This Derevenko is not the same one as my sailor-nanny.

"They do not know. They are doctors, da, but they are just men. Only God knows what the future will bring. You are young and strong. Mama believes you will get well. And you know it is always as the tsarina wishes. Now go to sleep."

The next day we visited a field hospital. Maybe Papa hoped this would change my mind about wanting to be a soldier. The place smelled of rotting flesh. But I didn't dare hold a babushka over my nose. It would have been impolite.

Papa walked on ahead. A soldier with a bloody rag around his head and a bandage on his bare chest reached out from his bed as I was passing by. He grabbed me by the edge of my uniform jacket so that I could not move.

Nagorny roughly batted the man's arm away.

"No!" I said to my *diadka*. "I will speak to this man."

I sent Nagorny on ahead, despite his protests.

"What is your name?" the wounded soldier said to me.

"Alexei Romanov."

"You are tsarevich?"

"Yes."

He laughed, then coughed, as if the laughing hurt him.

"I thought so. You excuse me if I do not get up and bow."

"How is your health?"

"Very good. Till I got this Hun bullet in chest. Wait—don't go."

His big hand closed over mine, completely circling my wrist.

"Skinny mal'chik. Are they starving you, too?"

I didn't answer.

"You will give your papa tsar a message?"

"Yes."

"Tell him, 'The people fight to the death for their tsar and Mother Russia. But at home time is running out.' Do you understand?"

The man suddenly fell back, looking pale and weak. He grabbed me by the sleeve again and whispered so quietly that I had to lean close to hear.

"Tell him . . . just that."

"'Time is running out.' I will tell him."

The man closed his eyes. And with a final, deep sigh, the steady rise and fall of his chest stopped.

CHAPTER SEVEN

BY THE SPRING OF 1915

our army had captured Przemysl, Austro-Hungary's strongest fortress. A month later we held most of the Carpathian Mountains. But when Germany came to Austria's aid with heavy guns, we Russians lost fifteen thousand soldiers in as long as it takes to go for a sleigh ride. When our soldiers retreated from Galicia, the servants said they heard Papa up pacing the floor half the night.

By the end of summer, Warsaw fell. And by the time leaves dropped from the trees, we had lost nearly one-and-a-half million soldiers in the war. Almost a million more had been taken prisoner. So Papa took over from Dread Uncle as head of our army.

Once the war began going badly, Mama sought help. She called for the one sent by God to save Russia and Papa. And that was how Father Grigory came back into our lives.

I was back in Tsarskoye Selo for a while.

"Ah, my dear boy!" my Cousin Felix said, as he saw me walking toward the mauve room. He hugged me a little too closely to his slender body, and I could smell his lavender perfume. "Up and about, I see, and looking charmingly innocent as ever. You really must come to my palace, and let your cousin Irina and me corrupt you!"

It was never easy to tell when Cousin Felix was joking.

"I have just come from seeing your friend Rasputin."

"Father Grigory?"

"Yes, but I prefer the name Rasputin: 'Debauched.' It suits him so much better, don't you think?"

He glanced from side to side to make sure nobody was near. Then he put his arm around my shoulders and led me to a corner next to a potted palm. Felix whispered and I felt his soft lips on my ear.

"Listen well, Alexei, for I will tell you this only once. When Rasputin has something to gain from you, you will have no finer friend in the world. But the moment you are no longer useful to him . . ."

Felix's finger slashed across my throat like a knife.

I gulped, then shoved him away.

"You cannot know him! Father Grigory, he is kind, he is generous," I said. "He helps me because he is a man of God! What—what could he possibly have to gain from me?"

"Not from you, perhaps. But from somebody else.

Someone who cares about you more than life itself, and who would do anything—anything!—for your sake. Take it from me, my dear boy. As cousin to cousin." Felix smiled and bowed slightly. "And if you ever find yourself in need of assistance, you know where to find me. The little yellow palace next to the Moika River. Where things people discard and have no further use for tend to wash up onshore."

With a grand sweep of his cape, and a final bow, like an actor finishing a performance, Felix left me alone on the stage.

CHAPTER EIGHT

IT ALL STARTED WITH A SNEEZE.

We have a saying that when the tsar sneezes, all Russia has a cold. And as you will see, this may be true of the tsarevich as well.

It was now December 1916, and the war had dragged on far longer than anyone had hoped. I was with my father again at general headquarters in Mogilev. I'd caught a cold the day before, and had a heavy catarrh in the head.

As we were leaving to visit regiments of the guard, I sneezed. This started a nosebleed. Papa had already gone on ahead without me. But for someone with my illness, a nosebleed is no simple matter. We tried rags and ice on my nose, but nothing worked. It was as if someone had opened a faucet in my head, and the red contents spilled out, along with my courage.

Papa was away, and Doctors Botkin and Derevenko

were back at Tsarskoye Selo. My situation was desperate. Professor Fiodrof could do little to help me. At last the professor sent an emergency telegram, calling Papa back to Stavka. My father came at once.

By the next day things looked hopeless. Gilliard bundled me onto the imperial train, taking me home to be cured—or to die. We sent our "dummy" train, the decoy, in the other direction to fool assassins.

Papa read urgent dispatches from the front in the forward car. But he kept coming back to my compartment to see if he still had a son. Nagorny held me propped upright in bed on the train. I remember little of what happened that night. But later I was told that twice I had fainted, and both times Gilliard was sure I was dead.

Mama and the girls met us on the train platform in Tsarskoye Selo the following morning. Mama was very relieved to see I was still breathing. My hemorrhage had slowed but not stopped.

"My darling boy!" Mama said on seeing me. "How I wish I could hold you! I embrace you not with my arms, but with my heart."

The slightest movement might start a gush of bleeding again. Nagorny carried me carefully into the palace, like a nervous apprentice chef carrying a thin-shelled egg. Mama put me in bed.

"We have no chloroform," Dr. Botkin said to Mama. "There is no time to waste. Give him vodka. And plenty of it."

She stared at him with wide, terrified eyes. Then she nodded, understanding what he meant.

Mama filled a tea glass with vodka.

"Drink, baby," she said, holding the glass to my lips as Dr. Botkin propped me up on pillows. "Yes, that's right. Quickly now. I know it tastes dreadful."

Vodka rushed to my head like a freight train. The icons on the wall spun in a blur of color, like my toy kaleidoscope. Dr. Botkin heated up a long thin metal poker in the fireplace. Nagorny held me down.

"Courage, my boy," Dr. Botkin said, bringing the white-hot poker toward my face. And suddenly I understood what they were about to do.

"No!!"

Desperate, I struggled to get away from them, but Nagorny and Derevenko held me down. Mama bit her lip in anguish, then turned away. She could not bear to look.

"Hold still, Alexei! Ouch!—he bit me!" Dr. Botkin sucked on his bleeding hand. "Grab him—before he gets away! You little fool! Do you want to bleed to death? It's for your own good!" Dr. Botkin said.

I bolted for the door. Nagorny caught me before I leaped out, pinning me against the door jamb with tattooed arms as big around as tree trunks. It was impossible to get free.

Defeated, I stopped fighting. Nagorny carried me back to bed and held me down once more. I braced for what was to come.

"It will only take a moment to cauterize the wound," Dr. Botkin said.

He brought the metal poker toward my face—closer, closer—my eyes widening in terror. Until the white-hot glowing point disappeared inside my nose.

Mama did her sad duty as she had so many times before. She stuffed rags into my mouth to muffle my screams.

CHAPTER NINE

THEY TELL ME FATHER

Grigory came to me several times while I drifted in and out of dreams. But I do not remember any of this.

When I finally awoke, it was nighttime. I was alone; it was dark. The servants had gone to bed. My throat felt like I'd swallowed buckets of sand from the Gobi. I could not call out. I swung my feet around to the side of the bed, and my toes scrunched up when they touched the cold floor. There wasn't enough blood in my head. It took me several tries before I could stay on my feet. The clocks all ticked together like the beat of army drums. I made my way unsteadily down the hall in search of water.

As I rounded the corner, I heard voices. Quiet murmurs—at first unclear. I wasn't supposed to be walking around by myself in the dark. I ducked behind a grandfather clock, then listened more closely.

"Such beautiful hands, God's work. Same God who

make poor Alexei and his troubles, make your hands perfect."

I recognized Father Grigory's voice. It got softer now, almost purring.

"This long white neck. Perfect. All the way from here . . . to here."

"Please, Grigory . . ."

The other voice. The voice of a woman. My mother!

"Come with me, Alix. Da, just for moment. Palace has many rooms, we find one empty. No one know but you and me. And God. All sacred in his sight."

"Please—don't—don't hold me that way. Nicky will . . . I—I must go."

Suddenly I heard my mother yelp. Her voice came out like a rabbit strangled.

"Stop! You're hurting me!"

Mama! Every inch of my weak body screamed out for me to help her. But I tell you, to my everlasting shame—I stood frozen like the Neva in January.

"Grigory promise to help boy again. Grigory keep promise. Now is time to keep yours."

I heard the sound of a body pushed roughly against a wall. And then a sharp slap.

"You dare strike a man of God?"

"Leave now!"

"As tsarina wishes. Da, I will let you go now, beautiful one. But sooner or later you must keep promise. Or you will be condemned before God and Holy Mother."

"No! You—you misunderstood. I promised you

STATON RABIN

nothing but kindness—and our gratitude. You know I cannot betray my husband. You must not talk like this!"

"You help Grigory. Or Grigory will help Alexei no more."

"What? You—but you must! My son will die if—"

"Grigory does not feel welcome here anymore. Grigory will not return."

I heard the sound of his heavy retreating footsteps.

"No—wait! Come back!"

Another set of footsteps, lighter, following his. Both came to a stop.

"Ah. Does tsarina wish to say something?"

"Please! You must come back."

"Bow to me."

"What?"

"Bow down! Kiss hem of my tunic, to show you are sorry. . . . Good. You kneel well. Are only woman, weak like any other. Beg me to stay!"

"Please—please, Father. I beg of you! Do not leave us!"

"And swear before the eyes of God you will keep promise to me. Now swear it!"

The sound of a woman's quiet weeping, and something mumbled.

"What's that? Do it, now! Grigory did not hear you."

"I said—I said, I swear."

"Da. Much better. Now stand. Stand and go, before someone see big tsarina weeping like little fool."

I heard my mother walking away, and then Father Grigory's footsteps, moving in the other direction.

My legs shook like our cook's gelatin mold.

Stepping out from behind the clock, I glanced down the hall in both directions. All was quiet. I was desperate to be alone—to think what to do. On wobbly legs I ran back to my room.

Breathing fast, I stumbled my way through the near darkness and sat down in my rocking chair. *LubdubLubdubLubdub*—each rock of the chair followed the rapid beating of my heart. I picked up the scarf I was making for Mama, and knitted, knitted—calming myself. *Lubdub, Lubdub . . .*

Suddenly the knitting needles were snatched from my hands. An arm gripped me tightly around the throat from behind, pressing on my breathing pipe.

"Twinkle, twinkle, little tsar. How I wonder what you are." The point of something sharp traced a thin line across my neck. "Friend? *Or enemy?*"

Father Grigory's rough hands released me. I gagged, then wheezed, gulping precious air into my lungs. I saw the glint of metal as he turned one of the knitting needles before my eyes. "I have always wanted to take up knitting. You don't mind if I keep?"

Frightened, I shook my head.

"Of course, one needle not much good by itself. Not useful for most purposes. But very useful for some others . . ."

I sat silent, motionless.

"Let's see throat."

He walked around to the front. I shook as he tilted my chin upward to examine my neck.

"Good. No finger marks, no bruise. Are you my friend, Alyoshenka?"

"Y-yes."

"And friends, they do not tell what overhear. They do not tell secrets?"

"No."

Father Grigory lifted me up in his strong peasant's arms, carrying me to bed.

"Maybe Alexei just imagine what hear anyway, da? Was just dream."

He tucked me in, kissing me on the forehead.

"Good night, Little One. Happy dreams."

CHAPTER TEN

THE NEXT DAY I KEPT TO MYSELF.
I was afraid that anyone who saw me could read
the torment on my face, and guess the reason for it.
There was a terrible war going on inside me, worse
than one with bullets or grenades: to tell, or not to tell.
But of one thing I was sure. Mama must never know
what I'd witnessed. If she knew that I too was in danger
from Father Grigory, it would kill her with worry.

I found my mother in her mauve room, resting on
a couch. She was reading one of her thousand books.
This one was the *Rubaiyat of Omar Khayyam*, love
poems she'd gotten as a gift several years before from
Papa. Mama forbade me to read the book till I got
older. But of course this only made it more fascinat-
ing, so once I had sneaked a peek at the inside. I saw
where Papa had written: "For my darling Alix Xmas
1912 fr. Nicky."

Mama peered over her reading spectacles as she

saw me enter the room. She closed the book with a *thunk*. How pale and exhausted she looked! Until then I had always thought it was her heart palpitations, headaches, and sciatica that made her too tired to get out of bed till noon. Or all those nights she spent awake, worrying about me. But now I knew how great Mama's sacrifice for my sake *truly* was—greater than I had ever imagined. She had something far worse to fear than any of us. And it weighed as heavily on her frail shoulders as the fate of Mother Russia weighed on Papa's.

"Ah, you are feeling better! Come, Sunbeam," Mama said, patting the corner of her chaise longue. "Sit by me and tell me a story."

"Are you all right?"

"Of course. Just a little tired . . . that's all."

I sat down next to her. As always, she smelled of rose oil, from the icon lamps in the master bedroom.

"Once upon a time in a land far away," I began, "Fairy Spring and Father Frost had a baby daughter. She was beautiful, and had eyes as blue as the Baltic, and pale white skin like snow. And she really was made of snow, which meant she was very fragile. So her mama and papa called her—"

"The Snow Maiden! I love that one. So different from my cold German fairy tales."

"And they hid her carefully from the Sun God, whose rays could hurt her. But the girl was very lonely, hidden in the forest. One day, the Snow Maiden decided to take a long walk in the woods. And after walking a long time, she heard beautiful music coming from a distance. She loved the music; she was drawn to it, and followed the sound. And soon she saw a handsome peasant standing in an open field—a shepherd, playing a flute."

"His name was Lyle."

"Yes. Don't interrupt me, Mama."

She raised an eyebrow, then nodded for me to go on.

"And the girl listened and watched him from under the shade of the forest trees. But she was jealous of all the other pretty girls who danced with Lyle, and who played with him in the open field. This broke the Snow Maiden's heart. So she walked home, and went to her mother and said, 'Mother Spring, how do I find real love?' Fairy Spring understood that her daughter was talking about the shepherd. So she said, 'You must leave the safety of the forest. You must go to the open field where the peasant boy who plays his flute can see you.'

"So the next day the Snow Maiden followed the sound of the music again. And it led her to the shepherd. He took one look at her and was enchanted. She was the most beautiful girl he had ever seen. Then the—"

"—the Snow Maiden stepped into a ray of sunlight," Mama picked up the story, "so the peasant could see her beauty all the more. But it was too much for her.

The Sun God's ray shone down on the Snow Maiden. And Lyle watched as she melted—melted, and was no more."

Mama sighed. "So beautiful, but so sad. Poor Snow Maiden. She is lonely, she leaves her parents and the land of her birth, and just when she's finally found love and happiness, it is all snatched away from her. And somebody she trusted very much betrayed her. Do you think it was her mama and papa, for advising her to leave the safety of the forest? Or the peasant, for luring her there with his snake charmer's music?"

"Um . . . I don't know, Mama. What do you think?"

She paused, blinking away tears, then replied: "I think that it doesn't matter who betrayed her. Happiness is fleeting and must be grabbed with both hands while it lasts. Even a brief moment of it can be worth all the suffering in the world."

I could not bear to see my mother unhappy. I could not bear the thought of anything terrible happening to her. I was ashamed of my cowardice. I was the future tsar of Russia, and must start acting like one! So I made my fateful decision. And may God forgive me for what I was about to do.

CHAPTER ELEVEN

I FOUND GILLIARD ON THE GROUNDS

of the Alexander Palace at Tsarskoye Selo, feeding apples to our elephant.

"Look at him, Alexei," he said, pointing to the great gray beast. The fingerlike end of the elephant's trunk wrapped around a big red apple and put it into his mouth. "He's standing up to his big wrinkled knees in snow, far away from his home and family, and may never see them again. The world is at war, the Russian people are on the verge of revolt. And he stands there calmly chewing his cud, like he hasn't a care in the world."

"You remember how you asked Papa to let me see more of the world?"

"Yes. His Majesty promised he'd discuss it with the tsarina. But that was a very long time ago, and I never heard anything more about it."

"I am older now. Please ask his permission again. I want you to take me to St. Petersburg. I mean, Petrograd."

"What's in Petrograd?"

I don't know how he managed it, but within two hours Gilliard had gotten my father's permission to take me to the city.

We knocked on the door to the yellow palace of the Yusupov family. A voice I didn't recognize answered.

"Yes?"

"It is Alexei Romanov, here to see his cousin Felix. With his tutor Gilliard."

The door opened only a little, and a tall man with olive skin and a bare, shiny muscled and hairless chest peeked out.

"It is impossible! Who are you, boy? The tsarevich does not travel without his family."

"He does now. Let me in."

The man frowned at me. Then suddenly he grabbed me by the collar and tried to throw me into the Moika River.

"Impostor!"

I fought like a hussar, swinging wildly, striking only the air.

Gilliard bravely joined the fray, battling the tall half-naked guard who carried a big scimitar in a scabbard and was twice his size.

"Are you mad?" Gilliard said between punches,

redirecting all the man's violence toward himself. "This is the tsar's son!"

Gilliard socked my assailant between the eyes, which made no impression on the guard. In return Gilliard got a good pop on the nose. The guard drew his sword, and just as he was bringing it down on Gilliard's head—

"Release him, Buzhinsky!" called out a familiar cheerful voice. It was Felix, coming to our rescue. "Buzhinsky" let Gilliard go—with reluctance, or so it seemed to me. The guard sheathed his sword.

"If the boy is injured—*even one hair on his head!*— the tsar will have both of you shot!" Gilliard said. "And I myself will pull the trigger!"

"Now, no need to make such a fuss, dear boy," Felix said, draping an arm around Gilliard's shoulders. Gilliard twisted out of Felix's embrace and scowled, rubbing his sore nose. "It was all just a simple misunderstanding."

Felix turned his attention to me.

"My apologies, cousin. You are always welcome here. But etiquette dictates that you should have told us you were coming. It's open season on grand dukes, you know, and Buzhinsky here was just doing his job—protecting me. Weren't you, Buzhinsky?" He petted his tall guard's bare arm muscles like he would a favorite dog, then turned back to us. "Let's go into my humble little palace, shall we?"

"What is wrong, Felix?" My cousin Princess Irina,

Felix's wife, approached us on cat's feet, a line of worry creasing her delicately pretty brow.

"Nothing, my dear," he said, not unkindly. "Just go back to doing what you do best: looking absolutely lovely." He gave her a peck on the cheek that seemed more like a kiss for a sister than a wife.

"Are you all right, Zhillie?" I asked Gilliard, using my fondest nickname for him.

"Yes. And you?"

I nodded.

We all went inside the house. Luckily, thanks to Gilliard's courage and quick thinking, the scuffle had left me completely unhurt.

Gilliard chatted with Irina downstairs in the parlor. That must have been a challenge for him, since though there was plenty to admire in her face, there was not much in her head. Meanwhile, I asked Felix to show me his collection of rare Chinese vases, upstairs.

"Now then," Felix said to me the moment we were alone. "Why don't you tell me what this little tête-à-tête is *really* all about."

"How did you guess?" He sat down next to me on the couch and tousled my hair.

"My darling Alexei. When a boy of twelve, who should be interested in girls, aeroplanes, and magic lanterns, suddenly develops a burning desire to see my Ming vases, I know that he is either going to grow up to be an interior decorator, or he has some particular reason why he must converse with me in private. It's about Rasputin, isn't it?"

I nodded. In a low whisper and a halting voice I told him all that had transpired. And when I was finished, Felix said: "Well, I can't say any of this surprises me. I warned you about him, did I not? Think no more about it, my boy. It's as good as done. Let's just say I have my own personal reasons, to put it delicately, for sharing your sentiments in the matter. Our nefarious friend the Mad Monk will trouble you and your good mother no longer."

"You will not hurt him? What do you mean?"

"Why, nothing more than to invite him to a little midnight fishing party at Yusupov Palace. With the fruit of the vine and your pretty cousin Irina as the bait."

CHAPTER TWELVE

IT WAS AFTER MIDNIGHT.

Gilliard had already left to see his brother who was visiting Petrograd and had suddenly taken very ill. Buzhinsky went home for the night, and my cousin's wife Irina had been sent to Yalta. I had been given permission to stay with Felix overnight at Yusupov Palace. Papa was reluctant to allow this, at first. But Gilliard reassured Papa by telephone that he and his sore nose could personally vouch for the palace's being well guarded. Papa gave in and said they would send a car for me early the next morning.

I was fast asleep in the small bedroom upstairs when Felix slipped into my room.

"Wake up, little prince," he whispered, gently nudging me. "''Tis now the very witching time of night, / When churchyards yawn and hell itself breathes out / Contagion to this world.'"

We went downstairs to the basement dining room.

A man wearing rubber gloves, whom Felix intro-duced to me as Dr. Lazovert, kept glancing nervously toward the windows. He nodded hello to me, and apologized for not being able to shake my hand. I watched as Dr. Lazovert put crystal powders into wine bottles and stuffed them into pastries. I noticed he left two of the pastries and one bottle untouched, and he pointed these out to Cousin Felix. Finally Lazovert removed the gloves and tossed them into the fire. The burning gloves made heavy, sharp-smelling smoke, filling the room.

"You fool!" Felix said to the doctor between rasping coughs. "Open the windows, before you kill us all!"

After the smoke cleared I stood before the blazing fireplace, trying in vain to warm the chill of forebod-ing in my heart. I sat in the dining room next to Felix, my cousin Dmitri, and another man, Purishkevich, who had arrived while I'd been asleep. Nobody would answer my questions. We waited.

At around one in the morning, through the win-dows at ground level I saw a black automobile pull up outside under a lamppost. A man wearing a light blue embroidered shirt and blue velvet pants got out of the car.

Father Grigory!

Felix grabbed me by the shoulder.

"The party is about to begin," he said. He told me that I could not attend but that if I hid behind the drapes at the top of the stairs, I would be able to hear all.

"Wait upstairs," Felix said quickly to Dmitri, the doctor, and Purishkevich.

I went upstairs too and hid behind the heavy drapes. Whatever was about to happen, I sensed it would not be something the tsar's son should be in the middle of.

From my hideaway I heard the familiar heavy tread of the Siberian peasant's boots as they crossed the marble floor. I held my breath, terrified he might hear me. Felix greeted him at the door. They went downstairs. Music began playing from a gramophone—an American song.

"Yankee Doodle went to town, a-riding on a pony . . ."

"So," I heard Father Grigory say to Felix. "Where is beautiful mare you promise: wife Irina?"

"Patience, my dear boy, patience," Felix replied, laughing. "You always were like a stallion champing at the bit! Our lovely Irina has been detained by unexpected guests upstairs but will join us for dinner shortly. In the meantime, have some Madeira. And these pastries—they're just marvelous! Irina made them herself, you know. "

"*Nyet!*" Father Grigory replied. "Too sweet. And no drink."

"Oh, please have some," Felix said, sounding nervous. "You will so disappoint my wife if you don't. And you don't want to disappoint her, do you?"

"*. . . Stuck a feather in his hat and called it macaroni. Yankee Doodle, keep it up. Yankee Doodle dandy. Mind* *the music and the step, and with the girls be handy."*

"I said, *nyet*! No time for this. Where Irina? I will go if she not here soon."

"Yes—yes, all right," Felix said. "Please don't go. I will go upstairs and see what is keeping her."

Felix took the stairs up, two at a time. He spoke in tense whispers to Dmitri and Purishkevich, while Dr. Lazovert joined Father Grigory downstairs.

"He won't try them."

"Why the hell not? Does he suspect?"

"No! I mean, I don't think so. You know Rasputin. He knows he is in constant danger, sees conspiracies everywhere. They say he even reads minds!"

"Try to talk him into it. Taste one yourself. Drink the wine."

"I tried that."

"Do you know which ones are safe?"

"Of course! Do you take me for an imbecile?"

Felix ran back down the stairs.

"Well?"

"I'm sorry, Grigory. My wife is just freshening up her rouge. You know how vain women can be."

"Only women? I seem to remember that you—"

Felix interrupted him. "Have a pastry?"

"Da. Nothing better to do while wait for crazy beautiful woman. . . . Mmmnnnn. Good."

"Please. Have two. There are plenty more where that came from. And here—it's even better with the wine."

"Da, *spasibo*. Two."

There was a long silence. As if they were waiting for something to happen.

"Would you—excuse me?" I heard Felix say at last. "I think I hear Irina calling me." He called upstairs. "Yes, dear! Right away!"

"Father and I went down to camp, along with Captain Gooding. And there we saw the men and boys as thick as hasty pudding."

I heard Felix's light footsteps running up the stairs.

"What now?"

"He ate, he drank."

"Good. Where do we take the body?"

"He's not dead."

"What? That was enough cyanide to kill a Hun regiment!"

"I tell you, he's fine! He just burped once, like a little indigestion. Now he's talking and laughing like nothing happened. "

"Did you give him the right ones?"

"Of course! Give me the gun, Dmitri."

"But, Felix, it will make noise!"

"Never mind. There is no one home to hear."

I wondered if Felix had forgotten about me.

Shaking with horror, I peeked through a hole in the curtains, and saw Dmitri remove something from under his cloak. Felix stuffed it under his dinner jacket, then ran back downstairs.

"*. . . Mind the music and the step, and with the girls be handy.*"

"I admire carpentry on your ebony cabinet here," Father Grigory said. "But who made?"

"Grigory Efimovich, you would do better to look at the crucifix and pray to it," Felix replied.

And then I jumped at the explosion of a gunshot.

CHAPTER THIRTEEN

DMITRI AND PURISHKEVICH

ran downstairs. My curiosity was stronger than my terror, and I followed.

Father Grigory, eyes shut, was lying face up in the basement on the polar-bear rug, its white fur now partly stained red. Felix stood over him, gun in his trembling hand. Our Friend's body suddenly jerked once or twice like a marionette, then was very still. I covered my eyes with my hands, as if somehow, somehow, I could erase this terrible picture from the photo album in my mind. *Holy Mother of God, what have I done? What have I done!*

Felix and the others trudged upstairs. Numb, I went with them.

"We must wait for it to get later to dispose of this business," my cousin said, "so there will be no witnesses." We sat in the parlor, but nobody had anything to say.

After the clock struck two, Felix went back down to the basement. From the top of the stairs I watched him press his fingers against the side of Father Grigory's neck.

"No pulse. Still warm," he said. He shook the body. There was no response.

As Felix turned away, I could have sworn I saw Father Grigory's left eye flutter slightly. Just slightly, like a butterfly's wing. But then I realized I had probably just imagined it. And anyway, Dr. Botkin had once told me that bodies often move for a little while after they are dead. *Dead!*

Felix started back up the stairs.

Like a furious polar bear, Father Grigory sprang to his feet and lunged at Felix with a roar. I tried to shout a warning, but no words came out. He pounced on my cousin with the strength of ten men, grabbing him by the neck and shoulders.

"What's going on down there?" Purishkevich shouted from the parlor.

Felix struggled mightily with Father Grigory. They knocked the table upside down. Crystal goblets crashed to the floor, spraying wine and glass against the paintings on the walls.

At last somehow Felix managed to tear himself from Father Grigory's iron grip. Then Felix ran upstairs, shoving me aside to get to the others.

"He's still alive!"

"What?!"

"The man is immortal!" Felix's eyes looked like they were going to pop right out of their sockets.

"Don't be ridiculous!"

Purishkevich dashed downstairs carrying a revolver.

"He's escaped!" Purishkevich shouted to us. "Jesus Christ! He's—he's running across the courtyard!"

I ran to the window. Father Grigory was stumbling across the snow in the moonlight. Stiff-legged, arms reaching out like Frankenstein's monster, the wounded holy man staggered forward. He fell, got up again, sprang forward—even stronger than before. Purishkevich bolted after him.

"Felix, Felix!" Father Grigory growled, as his blood left a jagged trail of red on the snow. "I'll tell everything to the tsarina!"

Purishkevich fired his gun, but missed. Then again—another miss. Purishkevich bit his own hand, as if trying to steady its shaking. He fired a third time.

Suddenly, Father Grigory's head bounced back, his body arching like Nijinsky's. He fell face-first onto the snow.

Slowly, head jerking, he rose to his knees.

Purishkevich caught up with him, and kicked him in the head. Father Grigory's arms and legs slipped out from under him. At last, he lay very still.

From the other side of the palace I heard a doorbell, then voices.

"Very sorry to disturb you at this time of night, Your Highness."

"Nonsense, my dear boy, you are always welcome. What seems to be the trouble, Officer Vlassiyev?" Felix replied with his usual charm. It would have taken an unusually smart man to notice the slight shaking in his voice.

"I was on my regular beat on Moika Street, you see, and I thought I heard several shots. Is everyone at the palace all right?"

"How kind of you to be concerned. That's what I like to see, a young man always alert, always doing his duty. It's a dangerous time. Yes, I thought I'd heard something too. It woke me from a delicious dream. But as you can see, it was nothing. All is quiet now."

"Yes. Probably just a car backfiring."

"Yes, that's likely indeed. Here's a little reward for your trouble."

"Oh, please, sir. That's so much! I couldn't possibly accept."

"Nonsense, it's the least that we can do, and far less than you deserve. Do come back for dinner sometime, Officer Vlassiyev. My lovely wife would be most happy to cook for a young man so devoted to protecting us."

"Why—thank you, Your Highness. That's awfully generous of you. Good night now, sir. Lock all the doors. Can't be too careful, you know, with all the lunatics about."

CHAPTER FOURTEEN

"OOPH! HE'S HEAVY LIKE AN OX!
Pssst—Felix!" Dr. Lazovert called. "Help us over here!"

Felix lifted Father Grigory's limp arm, and Dmitri, Lazovert, and Purishkevich took hold of his other limbs. They carried him into the palace and laid him near the stairs. Then Lazovert went back outside and shuffled the snow with his boot trying to cover the red.

Felix just stared down at Father Grigory. Lips moving, my cousin muttered angrily to himself as if remembering some long-ago conversation. Then suddenly he grabbed a dumbbell and smashed it over and over again against Our Friend's face and body.

"No!" I pulled at Felix with all my small strength. Somehow, of all the horrible and terrifying things I'd seen that night, this was the worst.

"Felix! Stop!" Dmitri said, pulling him off of Father Grigory. "Have you gone mad?"

Felix stood there with a strange gleam in his eye. Like a wild animal after a kill, splattered with blood.

Dr. Lazovert returned.

"Here's some rope from the toolshed," he said.

Lazovert and the others bound Father Grigory's arms together at the wrists, then tied his legs.

"That policeman who was here," Lazovert said, "do you think he will say anything to his superiors?"

"Go get him and we shall find out," Purishkevich replied.

Officer Vlassiyev stood by the stairs in Yusupov Palace, staring in horror at the mutilated body of Our Friend.

"Have you heard of Purishkevich?"

"I have," said the officer.

"I am Purishkevich. Have you ever heard of Rasputin?"

The policeman nodded.

"Well, Rasputin is dead. And if you love our Mother Russia, you'll keep quiet about it."

"Yes, sir."

Officer Vlassiyev was escorted to the door.

It was now almost dawn. Felix went upstairs to clean himself off. He was in some kind of daze. Talking to himself, laughing, and no use to anyone anymore. The others carried Father Grigory out to the car in a sheet.

"Come, Alexei," Cousin Dmitri said, motioning to

me. He was the first of any of them to address me since the brutal murder of Our Friend had begun. "You cannot stay here anymore."

It was very cramped in the car with the three of us. Four, if you count Father Grigory. I sat in the back.

"Where are we going?" I asked.

"To the Petrovsky Bridge on the Neva," Lazovert answered.

We hit a bump in the road. I felt a hand touch my shoulder. Someone was offering me comfort—thank God, how much I needed this!

I turned to look at the hand, and screamed.

It was Father Grigory's hand!

The sedan swerved, nearly going off the road into the river.

"He's—he's not dead!" I stammered. "His hand—it—it moved!"

"What? That's impossible! Look at him—a corpse if ever I saw one!"

I felt like I was going to be sick.

"Stop the car, Lazovert," Purishkevich said. "Check his pulse."

"I tell you, he's dead!"

"It was just the bump in the road, silly boy," Lazovert said to me kindly. "That's what moved his hands." He turned to the others. "There's no time to stop. It will be light out soon!"

† † †

We drove another verst or two, then stopped the car, hiding it behind some pine trees near the bridge. The Neva River was frozen solid.

"Here!" Purishkevich said, handing a heavy wrench to Dmitri. "Step out onto the ice and make a big hole."

"But it's still dark! I might fall through!"

"Shut up and do what I say!"

After the hole was made, they dropped Father Grigory's body through it. He sank slowly under the ice, disappearing into the dark waters. Going down, down—maybe all the way to hell.

"Leave the wrench behind, Dmitri, we don't want any evidence. Hurry up, Alexei!" Lazovert called out as he and the others piled back into the car.

"In a minute!" I shouted. I wanted to say good-bye, a real good-bye, to the man who had been Our Friend. I needed to be alone with him.

"I am sorry," I said to the hole in the ice. My tears formed crystals on my cheek. "So terribly, terribly sorry. You must believe me! I never knew it would come to this. You have children, I know. A wife. Dear God, what will Mama say?"

I reached inside my pockets. All I could find was a few kopecks, and my lucky Swiss franc, which Gilliard had given me. Shutting my eyes, I made a prayer, then threw the franc toward the hole in the ice. It made a *ker-plunck!* as it sank.

"God be with you, Father Grigory."

I turned to go. It was a long way back to the car. I trudged slowly up the riverbank, my heart and feet made of lead.

"Ouch!"

Something hard had hit me in the back of the head. Strange. I picked it up. A coin.

My coin.

I turned, knowing with horrifying certainty what I'd see.

"Father Grigory!"

"Twinkle, twinkle, little tsar. Now I know *just what you are.*"

He stomped toward me, blood and water dripping down his hand that held Dmitri's wrench. The rope, ripped in two, dangled from each wrist. His beard hung in icy black tentacles from his mangled face, like some mythical beast from the river. I tried to yell out, to run, but his voice had cast a spell over me.

"Don't dawdle, Alexei!" Dmitri called again from the car. They could not see us from there.

Step by bloody step, Father Grigory stomped toward me. I couldn't force my wobbly legs to move. Even if they could, I knew I wouldn't get far.

He was only ten steps from me now. Just ten steps till I met my *sudba*, and joined Grandpa Sasha in the other world. I shut my eyes and counted. *Odin, dva, tri . . .*

Holy Mother, have mercy on my soul. Please, take care of my family and Gilliard.

Chetyre, pyat, shest . . . Is it really true, Mama? That nothing hurts in heaven?

I pictured myself in a flowing red river, a place beyond pain. *Sem, vosem, devyat . . . desyat!*

I felt Father Grigory's cold wet hand grab me by the throat. I knew the wrench was raised over my head. I braced for the impact, my moment of death.

CHAPTER FIFTEEN

MOTHER OF GOD,
Blood of the tsar, I have no fear, Now take me far!

The words came back to me suddenly—like some miracle sent by Saint Serafim.

I waited for the wrench to strike my skull, but felt nothing. There was no pain. *Spasibo, Holy Mother!* Was I in heaven?

Then an icy chill ran through my body. I opened my eyes.

It was morning. Rasputin had vanished. Or maybe I had.

I found myself alone and shivering, carried along by the current in a freezing river, the water stained bloodred by a sunrise. But it did not look like the Neva. It did not look like any place I had ever seen before. And it was real, I was sure of it. Chunks of ice floated past my head. On both sides of the river I saw buildings, taller than any in Petrograd.

I dog-paddled furiously, trying to keep my head above water. I knew how to swim, but my limbs were weak. The undeniable fact was that I was drowning.

"Помогите!" I called out for help, waving frantically to a passing barge. "Помогите!"

But no one heard me.

My arms and legs were exhausted. My meager supply of blood froze quickly. I was sleepy, so sleepy. . . .

How cruel my *sudba*, to survive the day's many horrors—only to drown in the end! I tried to mumble a prayer, but my lips were too frozen to move.

And then at last, my strength was at its end. The frozen river took me into its cold embrace.

" . . . twelve, thirteen, fourteen, fifteen."

I felt something pressing again and again on my chest. Then soft lips, breathing right on mine.

I opened my eyes, and saw an inch in front of my nose the blue eye of a giant—the same one from my dream!

A girl giant, with long black eyelashes. When she pulled back, I saw she was just a normal-size girl. A little older than I, and more beautiful than an angel of God. She pressed her hands on my chest again.

"One, two, three, four . . ."

Coughing up water, I gasped for breath. I pushed her hands away and sat up.

"Меня зовут Алексей Романов. Вы говорите

по-русски?"‡ I said. She pushed me down.

"Look, dude, I don't know your language, but we gotta get you to a hospital, pronto."

‡"I am Alexei Romanov. Do you speak Russian?"

"Peasant, you don't speak Russian?"

"'Peasant'?" She put her hands on her hips. "Where are you from? Park Avenue?"

I grabbed her by the arm and spoke through cold-rattling teeth.

"No! C-c-cannot go to hospital! No one must know the ts-ts-tsarevich is ill."

"The who?" She took her coat off and covered me with it.

"I am Alexei Nikolaevich Romanov, son of Nicholas Alexandrovich, emperor and autocrat of all the Russias."

"Yeah. And I'm the Queen Mary 2. Just relax while I call 911."

She took a small metal square out of her back pocket and opened it up into a rectangle. I pointed to it.

"What is this?"

She just shook her head and touched the silver object a few times, then put it to her ear and talked to it.

"My emergency? I just pulled a kid out of the river; I need help.... Yes, he's breathing now. I did CPR.... Me? I'm fine. I didn't have to jump in to rescue him, he just washed up near the shore. . . . Suicide? I don't know. Maybe he just fell off a vodka boat. . . . I said a vod—oh, never mind! Just hurry up with the ambulance, okay? He must have hypothermia, he's talking crazy. . . . I'm near pier—"

I snatched the metal object away from her.

"Please! I beg you. It will mean the end of Mother Russia. Please—no hospital!"

I saw kindness in her eyes as they met mine. She sighed, then nodded, folding up the silver rectangle and putting it away.

"All right, it's your funeral. But I gotta get you warmed up. You're coming home with me."

CHAPTER SIXTEEN

"SEVENTY-NINTH STREET near West Side Drive," the girl said to the driver after she helped me into the backseat of the strange yellow automobile. There was a big pane of glass between us and the driver. He turned around in his seat and spoke to us through the glass.

"I don't want no drunks throwing up in my cab!"

"He's *not* drunk!" the girl replied.

"He throw up, you pay for mess!"

We drove through the streets of the city. All the signs were in English. But this place did not look like the pictures I'd seen of England.

"We are in America?"

"Last time I looked," she said.

"Conditions must be very bad here for peasants."

"What makes you say that?"

I pointed to a big poster on top of a tall building. It had a photograph of five beautiful ladies on it. I read to her the words on the poster: "Desperate Housewives."

She laughed.

"Da, you laugh now," I said, "but maybe they make revolution."

"I think they already have."

A little while later the automobile stopped at a building. I leaned on her shoulder as she helped me up the stairs.

"My mother's at work," she said, picking up a newspaper from the stairs, then opening the door with a key. "We've got to get you into some warm clothes."

I looked at the newspaper and stumbled. *2010!*

"Are you all right?" she said.

"What calendar you use in America?"

"Huh? The one with the hunky firemen on it. Why?"

I grabbed the sleeve of her jacket.

"Please! No joke! You must tell me. Nicholas is still tsar of Russia, da?"

She crossed her arms.

"You say you're his son. You tell me."

I showed her the newspaper.

"'Paris Hilton Caught in Sex Scandal,'" she read, shrugging. "So what else is new?"

"No—*this* one."

"'Russian President Visits U.S. to Discuss Chechen Problem.' So?"

"We have Chechen problem. We don't have president."

"You're shivering!"

The girl went went to a drawer and took men's clothing out of it. She returned to me.

"What are you doing?"

"Unbuttoning your shirt so you don't freeze your butt off, what's it look like I'm doing?"

I pulled away.

"You do not touch tsarevich. It is forbidden!"

She backed off and bowed low.

"Okay, Your Highness, King of Hypothermia. Suit yourself. You didn't seem to mind my touching you when I was saving your life."

"You save my life?"

"Yeah—like, duh!"

I felt myself blush. "You were kissing me."

"In your dreams!" she said. "I was doing CPR. You're, like, what? Twelve? Get real! Your voice hasn't even changed yet."

"CPR?"

"Maybe your alphabet is different where you come from and it's got different letters there."

"What is your age?"

"Old enough to be your big sister. I'm fifteen."

"My big sisters are older than you. I change clothes now. Turn your back."

She scowled at me and sighed, but turned her back.

I began changing into the clothes. They were too big for me, but they made me warm. I rolled up the pants legs so they would be shorter.

"Who belongs to these clothing?" I asked.

She did not reply.

"Who belongs?"

But then I thought I heard a strange sound coming from her. And then she said in a quiet voice: "Nobody."

"Look at me," I said. She did nothing, so I added: "The tsarevich commands it."

Slowly, she turned around to face me. Her eyes looked red.

"Vy ochen' krasivy."

"What?"

"I said, 'You are very beautiful.' Even when you weep."

I moved close to her and put a hand on her shoulder. She looked at me with grateful eyes. I spoke softly to her.

"I am very sorry to make you cry, Little Peasant. Thank you for saving my life."

CHAPTER SEVENTEEN

I NOTICED THAT THIS girl's emotions changed very quickly and without warning, like the weather in Moscow. Within moments her tears had dried up and her attention was focused on looking at a glass slide through a microscope, like the one that Dr. Botkin has. She scribbled notes busily on a page, as if she'd completely forgotten I was standing there.

"What is your name?" I asked her.

"Varda. Varda Rosenberg."

"You are Jew?"

"Yeah. You got some problem with that?"

"*Nyet.* Why were you at the river?"

"Homework. I was taking a water sample for my biology class. We're studying flagellates—to see how they survive colder temperatures in wintertime."

"Ah—you study Khlyst priests who beat themselves with tree branches? Why are they in river?"

"Not *flagellants*, flagellates! Tiny one-celled animals that swim using their tails."

"Da," I said, not really understanding at all. "You look at little animals now through microscope?"

"No, that's just for school. I'm working on something much more important—on my own. I'm looking at blood, under the microscope. Want to see?"

I shook my head. "*Spasibo, nyet.*"

"You all right? You look pale."

"Da—I—I am well."

"I'll tell you a secret. Not even my mother knows, she'd just say I'm crazy. I'm trying to find a cure for a disease. For hemophilia. Do you know what that is?"

I gulped and nodded.

"Hemophiliacs have a busted gene that won't instruct the body to make factors VIII or IX. Those factors are proteins that make blood clot so you won't bleed to death when you injure yourself. The disease often runs in families—it's carried on the X chromosome. Usually only boys have hemophilia, the girls are just carriers of the disease who can pass it along to their children." She noticed my puzzled look. "You're not getting any of this, are you?"

I shrugged. "I never hear of girl who have hemophilia."

"Yes, it's pretty rare," she said. "See, all people have inside their bodies something called chromosomes, and they inherit one type of chromosome—X or Y—from each parent. All boys have one X and one Y in each pair of their chromosomes, so boys are "XY." But girls have *two* X chromosomes in each pair—girls are "XX." Blood clotting factors are located only on the X chromosome. So girls get *two* chances to inherit a normal gene for blood clotting, since they inherit an X chromosome from each parent. And usually it takes only *one* healthy gene for clotting factors to prevent symptoms of the disease. That's why girls are hardly ever hemophiliacs—unless *both* their parents carry the defective genes for the disease, or there's a spontaneous gene mutation, which is pretty unlikely."

"Da?"

"But boys get a crummy break. They only have one X chromosome. So boys only need to inherit the hemophilia gene from *one* parent—their mother—to get the disease. That means hemophilia is pretty common in boys—about one in five thousand births. You've got that blank look again. Am I getting too technical for you?"'

Of course, I understood very little of what she was saying, but I shook my head and asked her a question.

"So. Is mother's fault boys are hemophiliac?"

"I wouldn't call it 'fault,' exactly—but, in a way, yes. Here, I'll draw you a picture. This is what happens when a normal, healthy guy marries a woman who carries the defective gene that causes hemophilia, and they have kids. . . ."

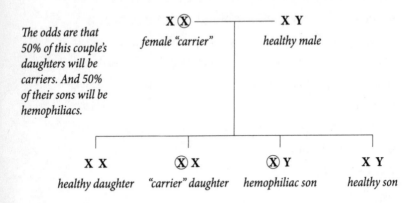

$\textcircled{X}$ = *Chromosome carrying the defective gene that causes hemophilia*

X $\textcircled{X}$ ——————— X Y

female "carrier"   *healthy male*

The odds are that 50% of this couple's daughters will be carriers. And 50% of their sons will be hemophiliacs.

X X $\textcircled{X}$ X $\textcircled{X}$ Y   X Y

healthy daughter   *"carrier" daughter*   *hemophiliac son*   *healthy son*

"I'm working on a new gene therapy treatment to cure the disease. Every person is born with about thirty-five thousand genes in their bodies, which are carried on their chromosomes. Stop me if you know this stuff."

I just looked at her, puzzled, so she continued.

"Genes give your body all the instructions for what you'll look like, what color your hair and eyes will be, what diseases you might get—maybe even what you will grow up to be."

"You mean like me growing up to be tsar?"

"Yeah, right," she said, in a tone that told me she still did not believe me. "No, I mean like what talents and abilities you might have. Intelligence, being good at playing the violin, things like that. That's partly

       STATON RABIN

something you inherit from your parents. Hemo-philia is one of only a handful of diseases that come from a defect in just one of those thirty-five thousand genes. We just have to fix *one gene*, and we've got it licked. I mean, scientists already know how to make white rabbits glow in black light by injecting them with genes from phosphorescent jelly-fish. So, in theory, curing hemophilia should be a no-brainer!"

She took a small glass bottle half-filled with clear liquid from a shelf and showed it to me.

"Now, here's a potential cure. This is adeno-associated virus, and scientists are trying to use this virus to help replace the broken gene with a healthy one. It's a virus that causes nothing—but it's similar to viruses that cause the common cold. So it's a good way to 'infect' somebody with whatever you put in it. See, first you take the genes out of this virus, then you plug in a healthy gene that will make blood clotting factors. Next, you inject the virus containing the healthy gene for factor VIII or IX into a hemo-philiac. And, presto! The virus replicates and carries the good gene throughout his body, making up for his defective one—and he's cured."

"A cure? Do you think is really possible?"

"Of course! At least that's the theory—I'm going to attend a science conference about this in about a week. But in practice it hasn't worked very well yet. Because most people's bodies react to a foreign virus by producing antibodies to it, and getting inflama-tion. A kid even died from gene therapy!"

"Oh. This is very sad that he died from . . . what you said."

"I'm trying to come up with a pill that can replace the damaged genes for factor VIII or factor IX so that the body won't reject the cure." She handed me a large pink pill. "Here's one of the prototypes. Of course, since it's only experimental, I can't test it on people—that's too dangerous, it's against the law."

"What made you interested in this bleeding disease?"

The expression on her face changed and she looked down at her hands.

"Someone I knew died of it."

"The man whose clothing I am wearing."

"Yes," she said.

"Your papa."

"Yes."

"I am very sorry to hear this. I can imagine how terrible it must have been for your family."

"No you can't."

Her words stung me, but I said nothing.

Varda shrugged, as if talking about this was not painful for her. But I was not fooled.

"Anyway, I was so young when he died, I barely remember him. He had the disease before they could make clotting factors through genetic engineering. Before the blood supply was safe. So he got AIDS from contaminated factor products."

STATON RABIN

"'AIDS'? You mean he got sick with some other illness?"

"Yes."

"You will be great woman scientist, like Poland's Marie Curie, da?"

"Well, maybe someday . . ."

I took her hand.

"Little Peasant, if anyone can cure this terrible illness of the blood, I believe you can."

"Thanks."

"Varda, there are some things about me I must tell you."

"Yeah, yeah, I know. You're the emperor of Russia."

"There is more."

"You're the queen of the Nile?"

"*Nyet*, no joke. Is important. I must tell you that—"

Varda looked at her watch, which had big numbers, no hands.

"Damn!—I'm already late for school. And I didn't even have time to do the reading for social studies last night!" She started stuffing papers into a bag. "We'll talk later."

"But, you must know that—"

"Later! Look, I can't leave you here by yourself. You'll have to come with me."

"No! I must go home! My mother is in much danger."

"In danger? Why?"

"Father Grigory—he may try to hurt her."

"You got a priest problem in Russia, too? Look,

after school we'll try to phone your family. Maybe they can wire you money for a plane ticket."

"Uh . . ."

She'd put on her coat and was already halfway out the door.

"Come on! I don't have time to gab."

CHAPTER EIGHTEEN

WE TOOK A STREETCAR

with no wires to Varda's school.

The girls at school had very short dresses and looked like painted ladies.

I kept trying to hold up my big pants that were nearly falling down. But the parents here must be very poor because all the boys' pants didn't fit them, either.

"God, we missed all of first period!" Varda said, looking at her watch as we hurried through the hall. "We'll make it to social studies, though . . ."

We saw a girl leaning against a wall, laughing.

"Hey, Blanche!" Varda said to her. "What'd I miss?"

"See that guy?" she said between laughs, pointing to a man whose back was to us. He was mopping the floor. "New janitor. He was cleaning the girls' locker room—while some of the uptown girls were still changing for gym! When they spotted him, the girls ran out of there, screaming their heads off. Pretty funny, huh?"

"Yeah, I guess. Did anyone report him?"

"Nah. Probably just an accident. He doesn't speak English very well—must have read his schedule wrong. Who's your cute friend here?"

"Just follow my lead," Varda said, whispering in my ear. She turned back to Blanche. "He's Alexei, my cousin from Russia. Alexei, this is Blanche."

"Da! Zdravstvuite!" I said.

"You'd better sign him up quick for ESL," Blanche said to Varda.

Before I could say anything more, Varda grabbed me by the sleeve and pulled me down the hall.

"Bye, Blanche, gotta run!"

Then she brought me to her teacher in a classroom. "Talk English," she whispered to me.

"This is my cousin Alexei, visiting from Russia," she told him. "Can he sit in on class, Mr. Brezhinsky?"

"Of course!" he said, turning to me. "We're studying your country now. I hope you'll tell us all about it— the kids will be really fascinated to hear from a native Russian. What part of the country are you from?"

"Tsarskoye Selo, near St. Petersburg."

"You live in the old *palace*?"

"Uh . . . he's the gardener's son," Varda said, hurrying me to a seat.

The teacher pulled down a map. I whispered to Varda.

"Name of country on map is mistake."

"'Russian Federation,'" she read from it. "Did they spell it wrong or something?"

Before I could say anything, the teacher spoke to the class.

"Okay," he said, "you all did the reading last night. Can anyone tell me when the Russian Revolution started?"

I raised my hand.

"Yes, Alexei? You're our resident expert."

"1905."

"Uh—well there was a revolution that year, but we're studying the one that came a few years after that."

I stood up.

"After? Teacher is wrong! Revolution was in 1905."

"Uh—he's just a little excitable," Varda said nervously to Mr. Brezhinsky, nudging me back down.

The teacher wrote some words on the blackboard: "Russian Revolution, 1917–1918."

When I left my homeland, it was December 1916. *Holy Mother of God! What had happened to my country? To my family?*

I whispered anxiously to Varda: "What is this—this Revolution 1917?"

"Hell if I know," she whispered back. "I didn't do the reading last night, remember?"

"You—you have Russian history book?"

"At home."

"Quiet back there!" the teacher said to us.

I sprang to my feet again.

"What happen in my country 1917? I command you to tell me!"

The class burst out in laughter.

"Oh, you do, do you?" Mr. Brezhinsky said. "Don't they teach this stuff in your school in Russia? And they could use a course in good manners, too, I think. . . . Well, if you'll just sit down and *listen*, young man, you might learn something. Can anyone tell me some of the causes of the revolution?"

I snatched a book called *History of Russia* off a boy's desk. But he made a face at me and snatched it back.

A girl at the back of the room raised her hand. The teacher called on her.

"The peasants and factory workers were starving and angry that a lot of them were dying in the war."

"Yes, Renatta! There's a girl who did her homework. What else? Varda?"

"I'm sorry, Mr. Brezhinsky. I didn't have time to do my homework last night."

"Well, two points for honesty, at least. Do it tonight."

He pointed to a very big boy who had raised his hand.

"Mitchell?"

"Tsar Nicholas II and his wife Alexandra were vicious murderers. They didn't care about the people's suffering."

I sprang to my feet and grabbed the boy by the throat.

"Liar!"

"Crazy Russian!" the boy said, pushing my hands away and grabbing me by the shirt collar. "Let's take this outside, paleface!"

Mr. Brezhinsky bolted toward us and pulled us apart.

"I won't have this in my classroom! Alexei—go to the principal's office! Now!"

"Please!" Varda said. "He won't do anything like this again. He's just got . . . ADD. He didn't take his Ritalin today. I'll be responsible for him—I promise!"

Mr. Brezhinsky shook his head at her, then stared at me and pointed to the door. "To the principal!" The teacher's ears were red with anger. "Down the hall on the right!"

Varda looked at me helplessly as I shuffled out the door.

CHAPTER NINETEEN

"THE BIG MAN AT SCHOOL— 'principal'—he says I am 'suspended.' This means what?" I said to Varda later that day.

"Wow! Suspended! After only one day—you must have set some kind of school record!" she said. "It means they won't let me bring you back tomorrow."

Varda and I were walking in a place she called "Rockefeller Center."

"I will not be here tomorrow," I said. "I must go home."

"Oh," she said, looking disappointed. "I know we've only known each other a short time. But . . . I will really miss you, Alexei."

"Me also."

"How will you get home?"

"I do not know. Maybe I cannot go back the way I came. I—"

She pointed to a big pine tree—the biggest one I had ever seen.

"What do you think of the Christmas tree? Pretty cool, huh?"

"Christmas tree?"

"Yeah, you know, like, Christmas? December twenty-fifth."

"Russian Christmas is not till January."

"Oh."

"I miss Christmas trees. We do not have them in Russia anymore. It is German tradition, and we are at war with Germany."

"At war with Germany?" she said, looking at me strangely. "Russia hasn't been at war with Germany since—"

I did not want to explain. I had been planning to tell her all. But now I feared that if I told her the truth about how I had come to be here, she would never believe me. I would have to tell her soon, but the time was not yet right.

Fortunately, she saw something that distracted her from our discussion.

"Oh, look!" she said, pointing to a big pit below the street. "The ice-skating rink! Come on, we'll rent some skates!"

"I am sorry, I cannot."

"You don't know how to skate?"

"Da. I know how. My sister Anastasia teach. But I must not."

"What are you, chicken? Don't be a baby!"

I did not know what to tell her. She shook her head, looking bitterly disappointed.

"Wuss," she said. She walked away from me.

"Varda! Wait!"

"Yeah?"

"I change mind. I skate with you."

Smiling, she walked back and pulled me by the hand. She borrowed the skates from a man in exchange for paper money, and quickly we were out on the ice.

I clung to the rail, watching her skate with joy in my heart.

"You dance like Pavlova!"

"Like who?"

"Great Russian ballerina. I have seen her dance at Mariinsky Theatre."

"Skate with me! You promised."

"No! I—It is forbidden!"

"I will help you."

Slowly at first, she cured me of gripping the rail.

"You don't mind if I hold your hand like this?" Varda asked. "I mean, you're not going to freak out on me again, are you?"

"*Nyet*. I do not mind."

I looked into her blue eyes, searching for my courage, and found it there. Holding hands, we spun around the ice together making circles. We danced together, like Nijinsky and Pavlova. It was like flying! I felt free—maybe for the first time in all my life.

"See!—you're a natural!" she said. "You're doing great!"

"What is this English word you use before: 'Wuss'?"

She laughed. "Never mind."

I laughed too.

And then it happened. The thing I had feared.

I fell on the ice.

I landed on one knee. I might be all right for a few hours, a few days. But I knew it was only a matter of time before the real trouble would begin.

Varda helped me up.

"Don't worry," she said. "Everybody lands on their butt sometimes. Even me."

We returned the skates. A sound made me jump.

"Your body—it—it is making music!" I said.

"Oh, that's just my cell," she said, reaching into her back pocket. "You don't have ring tones in Russia? That place is more backward than I thought!"

She talked to the metal rectangle again.

"Hi, Lanie. . . . Just ice-skating, with a guy who thinks he's ruler of the universe. . . . It would take too long to explain. Can I call you later? . . . Thanks."

She turned back to me.

"My friend," she said, pointing to the metal rectangle—as if that would make it less strange that she talked to it. She folded it up and put it away.

We walked down the street. I limped only slightly; Varda did not notice.

I saw something that made me stop in my tracks.

"What?" she said.

"It's—it's the man with muscles holding up the world! From my dream!"

She looked where I was pointing.

"Oh, that's the bronze statue of Atlas in front of the International Building. It's been there practically forever. You saw it in a dream?"

"Yes. I saw you in dream too. And you are more beautiful than I dream."

Varda blushed.

"Hey, Romeo, you're too young for me, remember?" she said.

"What if I told you I am one hundred and six years old?"

"I would say you're pretty spry for an old guy."

It was getting dark. We took the streetcar with no wires back to Varda's house.

"Thank you for this day with you," I said. "I will always remember. Even when I am one hundred and six."

"Me too."

"Varda, please tell me. What did your history teacher say in class about Russia after he sent me away?"

"Oh, I don't know, just some stuff about the 1917 Russian Revolution. You know: Rasputin, the

Romanovs, it was really sad. And how the Bolsheviks assassinated the tsar and the whole royal family in 1918—even the children."

My heart froze.

"Alexei! What's wrong?"

CHAPTER TWENTY

"STOP IT! JUST STOP IT!"

Varda covered her ears and shook her head violently. She wept. We were back at her home now, and I had told her everything. My whole story.

"I won't listen to this anymore!" she said. "You know—you know, I was really starting to like you. And then you lie to me, and start talking crazy again!"

"Is no lie! I am tsarevich. From 1916. You must believe me!"

"Look, I admit you look a little like the Romanov kid in my Russian history book, but so what? Lots of people look like other people! If I can prove you're not Alexei—I mean, without any doubt at all—will you stop talking crazy?"

"You prove? How?"

She showed me a book.

"My biology textbook. See this photograph? It's a DNA 'fingerprint'—that's a photograph of a person's genetic code. In Russia just a few decades ago some-body dug up some old bones. They thought the bones might be from Tsar Nicholas II and the royal family. Scientists tested the genetic code from the DNA left in the Romanov children's bones, and compared it to the code in living relatives of the Romanovs. They matched."

"I do not understand."

"If you are really a Romanov, your DNA—the gene code in your body—will be similar to the pattern in this picture. Do you believe me?"

"Da."

She showed me what looked like a big X-ray.

"See, here's my DNA 'fingerprint.' Everybody's DNA pattern is different—except identical twins—but people in the same family have similar patterns. I tested mine last week, so I'd have a 'control' pattern to compare other people's DNA to."

Varda looked me straight in the eye.

"If I test your DNA and prove you aren't who you say you are, will you shut up about all this Alexei Romanov nonsense?"

"Da, I promise. I trust you. But if you are wrong—"

"Then I'll bow down to you and believe everything you tell me. I'll need a DNA sample. Here—take this Q-tip and rub it around in your mouth. That'll collect some DNA from your cheek cells. Good. Now give it back to me."

She swished the cotton stick in a glass, and poured

in some liquids from several bottles. Then she picked up a glass beaker.

"Okay, now I'm pouring restriction enzymes into your DNA. That'll break up your DNA strand into smaller pieces. Then I dump the liquid containing your DNA strands into this tray of agarose gel. The gel acts like a strainer. The short strands of DNA will travel through it more easily than the longer ones."

She pulled a switch and I heard a machine noise.

"That turns on the electrophoresis. DNA has a slight electrical charge. The opposite electrical polarity in the tray will pull your DNA across the gel so that the strings line up in order of size. See? From shortest strands over here . . . to longest, over here."

Varda looked at me. "You're not getting any of this, are you?"

I shook my head.

"It doesn't matter. Talking out loud helps me remember the steps." She lifted a piece of fabric onto the tray.

"Okay, now I put this piece of nylon over the tray that holds your DNA. There's some absorbent material on top of the nylon, and that sucks up the image of your DNA pattern into the fabric. It's like a blotter. So we'll have an exact copy of your DNA pattern on the fabric. Like the image of Jesus's face and body some people say is on the Shroud of Turin."

She poured a liquid from a glass onto the fabric.

"Now I'm adding some special radioactive probes that'll stick to certain parts of your DNA pattern."

Varda put a black sheet on top of the fabric.

"This is X-ray photographic film. The radioactive probes that stick to key parts of your DNA will expose the X-ray film. There! Now I just put this sheet of film into the developer, and we wait till it's ready."

After a few minutes she pulled the X-ray film out. It had light and dark stripes, like negatives of photographs from my Kodak camera.

"Now we compare your DNA pattern bands to the picture in the book. Okay. Get ready to start apologizing."

She looked from one picture to the other, then back again. Varda's face dropped.

"But—but it can't be! The odds of this amount of similarity in the bands of DNA happening just by chance are only one in five billion! You're—"

"I told you," I said.

"Wait! Maybe—maybe I made some mistake in how I mixed up the restriction enzymes!" Varda said. "Where's my 'control' pattern? Ah, here it is!"

She picked up the other piece of developed negative film.

"Like I said before, this is my DNA pattern," she said. She compared her negative film to my pattern, and to the one in the book.

"Ohmigod!" she said.

"What is wrong?"

"You're Alexei."

"Yes, I know."

"But there's more."

"More?"

"You see the way your DNA bands here match these over here?"

"Da. So?"

" '*So*'? Alexei—we really *are* cousins!"

CHAPTER TWENTY-ONE

TO ME, IT ALL MADE PERFECT SENSE.

Father Grigory had told me that blood was like a river of time, joining everyone to their parents. And to their relatives yet unborn.

"Varda, it was not accident that it was you who saved me, pulling me from that river. It was our *sudba*, our destiny, to meet."

"Well, it figures," Varda said. "I'm related to a time-traveling lunatic from another century. But how the heck did we get to be cousins?"

"Varda, where did your family come from? Before they came to America?"

"From the Jewish ghetto—the shtetl. My family lived in Poland, in Warsaw. Which I guess was part of Russia, back then."

"They say my great-aunt, Princess Beatrice of England, had forbidden romance with Jewish artist from Poland. It make big scandal. Maybe this man one of your relatives!"

"Maybe . . . Wait!—My great-great-great-great-grandfather Isaac from Poland! There's a rumor in my family that he had a baby girl with an English princess who was a carrier of hemophilia. They fell in love while he was painting her portrait. Nobody in my family ever really believed the story was true. But that princess—she must have been your great-aunt Beatrice!"

"Da!"

"Their illegitimate baby was a big secret, so they gave her to a Russian family to adopt. I have a picture of my grandpa Isaac somewhere. . . ." She pulled a photo album out of a drawer and flipped the pages. "Here! See?"

"Good-looking *mouzhik*."

"And here's a baby picture of Isaac's granddaughter: my great-great-grandma Tillie from Russia. She looks like both of us!"

"*Kuzen* Varda, you must help me get home. You must help me save my family. They are in terrible danger!"

"What do you expect me to do?"

"I will need help. You must go with me."

"With you? Back to the Russian Revolution?"

"Da."

"Look, I like science, but I don't mess around with anything that burns, explodes, or might leave me stranded in a revolution in another century. Hell, I won't even eat genetically modified cornflakes! It's your problem, you deal with it."

I took her hand.

"My family is your family also."

She just shook her head.

Suddenly I winced and moaned with pain, gripping my knee.

"That's where you fell on the ice!" she said, reaching for the leg of my trousers. "Here. Let me take a look at that."

"*Nyet*, is all right." I pulled away from her.

"Let me see," she insisted. She rolled up my pants leg.

"My God, Alexei! Your knee is swollen up big as a baseball. What's wrong with you?"

"I am like your father," I said.

"You have AIDS?"

"*Nyet*. I do not know this 'AIDS.'"

"You mean—You're a hemophiliac? And you went *ice-skating*? For God's sake, why didn't you tell me you were sick?"

"I—I try to tell you. But we were having such good time."

"Alexei, we've got to get you to a hospital for an infusion of factor VIII before you bleed to death."

"No! My illness is secret!"

"It doesn't matter now. It's 2010, nobody knows you here. If you keep this 'secret,' you're going to be one dead tsarevich!"

We heard a sound at the door.

"Oh, no! My mother's home!"

CHAPTER TWENTY-TWO

"VARDA, WHO IS THIS BOY?"

Her mother stood there in the doorway, staring at us.

"He's—Alexei," Varda said, turning red. "Uh . . . our exchange student! From Russia."

"What do you mean, 'our'?"

"I—wanted to surprise you. Things have been kind of lonely around here since—well . . . The school psychologist said he would be good for my emotional development."

"So you went and ordered up a live-in guest without telling me?"

"Mom, it's only for a day or two!"

Varda's mother turned to me.

"Excuse me, young man, do you speak English?"

"Da. I mean, yes, thank you, Varda's mother."

"Look, this is not about you. You seem like a very nice, polite exchange student, okay?"

"Thank you. Gilliard says I must learn humility. I try this."

"Okay. I don't want to scar you for life or cause an international incident. But would you kindly step out into the hall for a moment so I can speak to my totally insane daughter in private?"

I sat outside in the hall. I could hear them arguing through the door to Varda's room.

"Varda!—What were you thinking?! Have you been doing anything with that boy that we had one of our talks about?"

"No, Mom!"

"Well, thank God for that at least. Are those Daddy's clothes he's wearing?"

"Yes. But—"

"Varda, how—how could you!"

I heard the sound of weeping.

"Don't cry, Mom. I'm sorry—really. But we didn't have anything else for him to wear! He was freezing when I pulled him from the river, and—"

"From the river? I thought you said he was an exchange student!" I moaned with pain and gripped my knee. "You hear him out there? He's crying! God, now I've upset him and—and he's going to go home and tell the Russian president that Americans are monsters!"

"No, that's not it! Mom, he hurt his knee. He's got hemophilia."

"Hemophilia? Varda, you've adopted a hemophiliac exchange student?"

Varda's mother took us in her automobile to the hospital. Everything was very white and clean there.

"Health insurance?" a woman said, sounding like she found her job very tiresome. She was sitting behind a little glass window in a room with a sign that said: ER.

"Uh . . . I don't think he's got any, Mom," Varda said.

"Write down: 'none,'" her mother said.

"Are you his mother?"

"No."

"Will his parents be responsible for the bill?"

"Da!" I said. "They pay to build many hospitals in Russia!"

"How lovely. Parents' names and employment?"

"My father is Nicholas Alexandrovich Romanov, head of—"

"—A very big multinational corporation," Varda interrupted.

"Which one?" the lady asked.

"It's in Russia, you wouldn't have heard of it."

"Try me."

Varda looked at me helplessly.

"The Mariinsky Theatre," I said.

"That's a big multinational corporation?"

"Uh—yeah!" Varda said. "His parents own a whole chain of theaters. It's like Loews!"

The lady gave us a strange look and scribbled it down.

"Okay, you're registered," the lady said, sighing. "Sit down over there in triage and wait till you're called."

I was lying on a narrow bed that had wheels. The nurse stuck a long needle into my arm and I wrinkled up my face. She paid no attention to me, and combined a clear liquid from one small bottle with the powder from another, and drew the mixture up into a big syringe. I felt a strange coldness inside my arm, and realized that she was slowly injecting the solution into it through the needle. Varda told me that they were putting factor VIII into my vein, to stop my bleeding.

"He'll be fine. The treatment will take only about fifteen minutes," the nurse said, turning to Varda's mother. "But he has to come back tomorrow for another infusion. It's important."

Varda's mother nodded. "We know the drill."

Soon, they went out into the hall to talk, while Varda stayed with me.

"How do you feel? she asked me.

"Dizzy, at first. All right, now."

"Does your knee hurt much?"

"I am used to it. All my life, has been like this for me."

"I know. It was like that for my dad, too. He was brave. I never heard him complain."

"I thought you said you did not really remember him?"

"I remember."

"Will you miss me too when I am gone?"

"What do you think?"

"Maybe a little?" I said.

"Maybe more than a little. Please don't go, Alexei! Look at you—you can barely walk! My history teacher said your whole family got killed by the Bolsheviks in 1918. If you go back to the Russian Revolution and can't save your family, you'll be killed too!"

"Is so. But my family has always helped me. And I swore to Holy Mother and to my mama and papa that I will always take care of them. My family need me. Mother Russia need me. I am tsarevich! I must try."

She shook her head. "I don't think I could be as brave as you."

"You were brave to rescue me."

"Everyone is brave when they have to be."

"Da. So you understand why I must go home and try to help my family."

Varda sighed.

"Yes," she said.

There was a long pause.

"Alexei?"

"Da?"

"I've changed my mind—I am going with you."

"What? The tsarevich forbids it!"

"Wait a minute! I thought you told me this afternoon that you *wanted* me to go with you?"

"I change mind too. You were right—is too dangerous! Besides, you are just female!"

"Yeah, and you're, like, what? A skinny hemophiliac boy who has lived in a palace with servants
waiting on him all his life and can barely take care of
himself! What if you bump yourself again and can't
walk? I know medicine, and I'm another pair of legs.
I can help you!"

I did not know what to say to her. What she said
made much sense.

"Please, Alexei! Let me help you."

"All right," I said at last. "But are you certain? It will
be very dangerous, Little Peasant."

"I know. I don't mind."

"I have one question."

"Yes?"

"We have known each other only one day. Why
would you risk life to help me?"

"That's easy," she said, smiling. "We're cousins. And
blood is thicker than water."

CHAPTER TWENTY-THREE

"YOU ARE LOOKING MUCH BETTER, ALEXEI.
And your knee swelling has gone way down."

"Da. Am feeling much better."

It was nighttime. I was in bed in the guest room at
Varda's house, with an ice pack on my knee. Varda
was sitting in a chair beside me. From the window we
could see the river sparkling in the moonlight.

"What do they call river?" I asked.

"The Hudson. After the man who discovered it,
Henry Hudson."

"Is beautiful in moonlight. Like Neva River. . . . And
like you." She blushed. "You will like Neva."

"I'm sure I will."

We watched the river together for a while. There
were a few boats sailing on it.

"Hmmm. . . . Didn't river flow in other direction
this morning? Or do I imagine?"

"No, you don't imagine. The Hudson is really an

estuary, not a river. So it's pretty weird. Every six hours or so the current changes direction. My science teacher said the rising current—the flood tide—flows north toward Troy. The ebb current flows south, toward the sea."

"Very strange." I shrugged. "Where is your mama?"

"In the other room. Asleep."

"Good. Won't she worry when she wakes up tomorrow and finds you are gone?"

"I left her a note. I told her the truth: that you're Alexei Romanov, the heir to the Russian throne, and we're going back to 1918 to try to save the royal family from being assassinated. Alexei, we really should go back to the hospital here first, to get the rest of your factor VIII treatment."

I shook my head. "No time! My family is in danger. We must go now—or it may be too late!"

"But your treatment will wear off by tomorrow morning! If you bump yourself again . . ."

I stood up carefully on my sore leg and took her hand.

"No time for hospital! Are you ready?"

Varda took a deep breath, then nodded.

"Shut your eyes."

I counted: *"Odin . . . dva . . . tri . . . chetyre . . . pyat . . . shest . . . sem . . . vosem . . . devyat . . . desyat!"*

I imagined the red river of time, flowing in my mind.

"Now, Varda, say after me: Mother of God . . ."

"Mother of God."

"Blood of the tsar . . ."

"Blood of the tsar."

"I have no fear . . ."

"I have no fear."

"Now take me far!"

"Now take me far!"

We waited.

Nothing happened. We were still right where we'd started.

"Is not working."

"Are you sure you didn't get the mumbo jumbo wrong? Maybe you're supposed to click your heels together three times or something."

"You think I am fool? Did not make mistake!"

"Okay, okay! Don't bite my head off!"

I counted to *desyat* and we tried again. Still: nothing!

"Is never going to work! Is like Father Grigory said! I must travel only with mind, not with body. If I travel with my body, he warn me: I will never return!" Varda put an arm around my shoulders. "I will never see my family again!"

"I'm sorry, Alexei. Really. Please don't cry! I know you wanted to help your family. Maybe you'll still find a way. But to tell you the truth, I'm kind of relieved. Now you can stay here where you'll be safe."

Just then the door sprang open.

Varda's mother was standing there in her robe,

with one hand on her hip, eyes blazing. She thrust forward a piece of paper that she was holding in her hand.

"Varda Ethel Rosenberg, do you care to explain this little note you've left for me?!"

"Uh—it's—it's just a history project, Mom. Mr. Brezhinsky said to pretend we could travel in time, and—"

"Save it!" Varda's mother said, holding up her hand. "I'm going to have a nice, long sleep. And when I wake up tomorrow morning, my daughter will have miraculously regained her sanity! Is that clear?"

"Good night, Mom, don't worry."

Varda's mother turned and shuffled back down the hall, shaking her head.

"Wake up, Your Highness." It was the next morning, and Varda had come into my room and shook me from sleep.

"Huh?"

"Listen, I've gotta go back to school today. You're not allowed to go with me, remember? Just stay here, so you don't get into any trouble. My mother will take you back to the hospital later. I'll meet you here after school." She handed me a metal rectangle.

"This is a telephone. It's lightweight to carry around, but superstrong—it's made of Kevlar, the same stuff they make bulletproof vests from. Look, you can use this to reach me anytime you want. You listen here, and you talk here. Just press this button and it'll ring the spare phone I've got on me. You know—'telephone'?"

"*Of course* I know telephone! I am not from Stone Age!"

"All right! I was just checking. Look, I'm trusting you with my own phone because it's easier to use than the spare. Just don't jump into the river with it."

"Hah! Very funny. Romanov family trust me some-day to run whole country. I think you can trust me with telephone." I pointed to a symbol on it. "What is this here? Three letters and two ladders twisted together."

"It's my personal icon: my initials—*V-E-R*—plus a double helix, the symbol for DNA."

"*Icon?* You mean like holy icon?"

"Uh . . . not exactly. It's more like my signature so I know it's my phone. I'll leave both phones' video switches on. When you call me, I'll see a moving pic-ture of you, and you'll see me talking too."

"Everyone here walk around with telephone! Why do you stick like glue to telephone?"

"Somebody may be trying to reach me. It could be something important."

"Someone always trying to reach my father. *He* does not walk around with telephone. You are more important than tsar?"

"Listen, we'll talk about that another time. I'm going to be late for school. One more thing: This phone is also a text messenger. You just type in words on this little keyboard, press this button, and I will receive them. Like sending a letter. Okay?"

I nodded. She handed me a piece of paper.

"Here's a list of text message codes. It'll give you short ways to type certain words. It saves time and money. Uh . . . I mean, rubles."

"Da. Time and rubles. Good."

I looked at the list.

"'IMHO' mean 'in my humble opinion.' 'ILUVU-WAMH' mean 'I love you with all my heart.'"

"Right," Varda said. "Memorize that list. I gotta go; I'll see you tonight."

I tapped out some letters on the little telephone: ICU2NITE. "Is almost like typewriter I have at home!"

"Great! You're getting the hang of it!"

After Varda left, I went into the other room and sat at the eating table. Her mother came into the room carrying wet clothing.

"I found this in the hamper. Alexei, is this your . . . uh . . . uniform?"

"Da. Hello, Varda's mother."

"Please—call me Mrs. Rosenberg. Wow! All you kids dress like rock stars these days. Well, I'll just put these clothes in the dryer. What do you want me to do with the medals?"

"You keep. I have no use for them now."

"Uh, thank you. That's very thoughtful of you, Alexei. But I think you should keep them. By the way,

I left some clothes for you on the chair outside your room—I borrowed them from a neighbor boy who is about your size."

"*Spasibo*."

"How are you feeling?"

"Better. Bed is soft. Better than home. I sleep on metal army cot at home."

"Army cot? They are drafting twelve-year-olds in Russia?"

"*Nyet*. But I go with my father when he is with army."

"Your father is in the army?"

"My father is head of whole army!"

"Really. And he finds time to run a chain of movie theaters, too. You know, we really must telephone your parents. They must be terribly worried about you."

"Da. And I worry very much about them. But your telephone will not reach so far."

"Homesick?"

"Excuse please?"

"I mean, you seem very sad. Are you missing your home?"

"Da. Very much."

"Where's Varda?"

"She left already for school," I said.

"Without you?"

"I am suspended. I am very bad exchange student."

"Oh, I wouldn't say that. Can I get you some breakfast?"

"*Nyet*. I am not hungry."

STATON RABIN

"Please—you must eat!"

"All right. Blinis. Borscht."

"Uh . . . How about bacon and eggs?"

"Good. *Spasibo*, Mrs. Rosenberg."

"You're so polite! That's so rare in a young man these days."

She mixed up some eggs for me at the stove.

"Mrs. Rosenberg, is Varda healthy?"

"Healthy? You mean, does she have hemophilia?"

"Da."

"No, she doesn't. But she's a carrier because her father had the disease. Why do you ask?"

"I wonder if she have healthy children."

"Oh. Well, we can't know for sure in advance. Do you want to marry my daughter?"

"Even more than I want to be tsar! Why do you laugh?"

"I don't mean to laugh. Here are your eggs. . . . Slow down, Alexei! You eat like you haven't eaten in a century!"

"It is very difficult to have family that is sick, da?"

"Da," Mrs. Rosenberg said sadly. "It was very hard on Varda when she lost her father. I don't think you ever get over something like that. I—I try not to lose my temper with her—I do! Really. But it's been very hard on me, too. Sometimes—sometimes I think I'm a terrible mother!"

She put her head down on her arms and wept. I didn't know what to do. I patted her on the hand.

"Mrs. Rosenberg, I do not think you are terrible mother. You are good mother to me."

She looked up at me with grateful eyes.

"*Thank you*, Alexei," she said, wiping her tears. "And, Alexei?"

"Da?"

"I think you are a *very* good exchange student."

CHAPTER TWENTY-FOUR

I STOOD IN MY ROOM

at Varda's house, looking in the mirror at myself. The clothes her mother had borrowed for me were very strange. There was a little fabric tag sewn inside the shirt that said: LANCE ARMSTRONG. The mother of Lance, the boy who owned these clothes, must have sewn his name into them so he wouldn't lose them. The shirt had a word on the front in big letters: LIVESTRONG—spelled backward in the mirror. But the shirt and trousers fit as well as if they'd been made for me by our imperial tailor.

I looked at the titles on Varda's shelf of books. Tolstoy's *Anna Karenina*. That one, of course, I knew before. But: *Captain Underpants*? *Sisterhood of the Traveling Pants*? Lots of Pants. *Rich Dad, Poor Dad*. That one must be about revolution. Hmmm. . . . *The Slow-Carb Diet*. I wondered if the Diet in the city of Slow-Carb was anything like our Duma.

Not knowing how else to occupy myself, I sat down in a chair and stared at the wall. Thoughts came to me that I had tried so hard to push from my mind. *What in the name of Saint Serafim would my family think had happened to me? What would Cousin Felix tell them?* Certainly not the truth! That he had poisoned and shot Father Grigory, and I mysteriously vanished when they were dumping his body in the icy Neva. My poor mama and papa would be half-crazy from worry about me! They'd think Felix must have killed me, too!

Where would the revolutionaries take my family? Would they hurt them—God, I pray not *torture* them!—before they killed them? What would these cruel beasts do to my beautiful sisters? The Bolsheviks and their like! They had thought nothing of blowing Great-grandpa Sasha to bits—and Uncle Serge, too! They would stop at nothing—*nothing!*—to destroy my family. And I had no power to save them!

I looked out the window and watched the boats going calmly by on the gently flowing river. A world away from the Neva. A world away from my world.

Suddenly an idea came to me. Hand trembling with excitement, I pushed the button on Varda's telephone. Her voice answered, and her pretty face appeared on the telephone's little screen.

"Hi, Alexei. What's up?"

"I think I figure out how I can return home!"

"Huh? I can only talk a minute. I'm in the school

basement, and my cell might cut out. I'm waiting for the janitor. We had a great talk at lunch yesterday after you left school. He was really curious about you, because you both come from Russia and he saw us together."

"Da?"

"I promised him I'd look over some boxes of chemicals in the basement for bio class today and tell him which ones are safe to store near the heating pipes. What did you need to tell me?"

"Varda, I look at river today, and is flowing backward again!"

She sighed.

"Is *that* all? I already explained that to you. It's an estuary. I gotta go—"

"*Nyet!* Don't you see? Hudson River can flow both directions. *Maybe so can river of time!*"

"What do you mean?"

"If I imagine red river in my mind flowing other direction—*backward*—maybe it will take us *back* in time to my family!"

"Alexei—are you sure?"

"*Nyet.* But we must try! Come home, Varda. Now!"

"I can't come now. Mr. Efimovich will be here any—"

"*Efimovich?*"

"I told you—the new janitor. What's the matter? You look as pale as—"

The phone dropped from my hand. I picked it up and put it back to my ear.

"Varda! You still there?"

"Yes."

"You must tell me! Quickly! What does this Mr. Efimovich look like?"

"What difference does—"

"Please, Varda! Is important!"

"Well . . . a little weird, actually, but he's a nice man. He's got this long, ratty-looking dark beard. His face has scars all over it—he told me that he was in a terrible plane accident. And his eyes . . . well, they're hard to describe. But when he looks at you, they seem to be staring right into—"

"Varda, leave basement immediately! Do you hear me? *Now!*"

"But—"

"I command you to leave! You are in danger!"

"Don't be silly!" Varda's face looked annoyed. "You 'command' me, do you? Well—"

Varda's face disappeared from the telephone's little screen. I heard a muffled scream.

"Varda? *Varda!*"

"Twinkle, twinkle, little tsar . . ."

Mother of God!

CHAPTER TWENTY-FIVE

FATHER GRIGORY'S MANGLED FACE, like a grinning demon from hell, replaced Varda's on my telephone screen. He threw back his head and laughed till his gold teeth showed.

Then the screen went black.

I limped as fast as I could toward the door and down the hall.

"Alexei! Where are you going?"

"I am sorry, Varda's mother! I must go!"

Outside I waved frantically to those yellow automobiles that had taken me to Varda's house. Many went by. They would not stop for me.

"Stop!" I shouted as another one went by slowly. "I am Tsarevich Alexei, heir to the Russian throne!"

The automobile stopped.

I limped to the front door where the driver sat. The man rolled the half-open window all the way down.

"*This* one," the driver said, shaking his head, "I gotta hear. Get in, kid. Where you want to go?"

"Bring me to Varda's school! She is in danger! Hurry!"

"Listen, buddy. There are twelve hundred public schools in New York. Work with me here. Which one?"

"I do not know."

The driver shook his head. "Sorry. Can't help you."

He started to roll up the window.

"*Nyet!* Wait! School was called P. S.!"

The driver shook his head again. "Sorry, kid. *All* of them are P. S. Gotta go." He rolled the window all the way up.

"Please, do not go!" I shouted through the window as he started to pull away. I pounded on the window. "I remember—school had number on building!"

He stopped the car. "Huh?" The man couldn't hear me.

I held up the fingers of both hands.

"P. S. 10?"

I nodded my head up and down quickly many times.

He rolled down the window.

"Okay, kid, that's more like it. Get in."

We stopped in front of Varda's school.

"Look, buddy, I know New York is the melting pot and all." He looked at the coins I had handed him. "But I got no use for this kind of money."

"Is all I have! Kopecks is good money!"

"Yeah, I'm sure it must be good someplace. But it ain't any good here. Pay up or I'm taking you down to the police station."

"Police? No, please! I must go! My friend is in danger! My father will pay you. He has bank account in England, can get American money!"

The man sighed. "All right, kid. Write down his name and address on this pad."

I did what the man said, then hobbled quickly up the stairs of the school. As I opened the big metal doors, I heard the driver shouting after me.

"'Emperor Nicholas II, Alexander Palace, Tsarskoye—' *Hey!* Come back here!"

I limped quickly down the hallway, and ran right into a girl who was carrying books in her arms. The books tumbled to the floor.

"Watch where you're going, you dweeb!"

I helped her pick them up.

"Sorry! Where is basement?"

"Down there," she said, pointing.

I scrambled down the stairs.

"Alexei!" I barely heard Varda's strangled shout.

Father Grigory's arm was wrapped tightly around her throat. Her eyes sent out a desperate plea for my help.

"*Dobryi den'!*" Father Grigory said to me calmly,

bowing his head slightly. "You must be tired. Sit down, make comfortable." He pointed to a chair in the corner of the basement. "Young lady and I expecting you. You forgive if we have no plate of bread and salt to welcome tsarevich."

"Let her go!"

"Patience, Alyoshenka, patience. Not just yet." He ran his finger down Varda's cheek. "I am enjoy conversation with this pretty girl."

"If you hurt her, I'll—I'll—"

"You will—what? Guns and poison do not finish off Grigory. But you? Pinprick is enough to kill Alexei! Right, pretty girl?"

He squeezed her neck more tightly. Varda made a noise like she was choking.

Desperate to help her, I stumbled toward them.

"Take off socks and shoes," Father Grigory ordered.

"*What?*"

"Do what I say!" Father Grigory ordered. "Or pretty girl's face not be so pretty anymore."

Keeping one eye on him and Varda, I took off my socks and shoes and tossed them aside.

With his free hand Father Grigory reached inside an open cardboard box.

He grabbed a few glass chemical bottles.

SMASH!

He shattered the bottles on the hard cement floor.

I cringed, trying to protect my face and eyes.

CRASH! SMASH!

"You want to save pretty girl? Go ahead! They say the fakirs in India walk across hot coals. Let's see tsarevich walk across *this*!"

He threw more and more bottles, until the whole floor between me and Varda was an ocean of broken glass.

"Let her go! I am your sovereign. In the name of the Russian crown, I command you!"

Father Grigory made a clucking sound with his tongue. "You forget, Alyoshenka. We are in America, now. Land of free, where even humble peasant from Siberia can rule! You are not tsarevich here."

"You want to kill me? Let go of Varda, and you can have me!"

"Ah!" Father Grigory said. "A trade—like rabbit for mule. It is deal! Are you mule? . . . Or are you frightened little rabbit?"

There was no time to listen to my fears. I knew what I had to do. I took the first steps toward them across the field of broken glass.

"Alexei—don't! You'll bleed!" Varda said.

But I kept on walking—slowly, step by unbearable step. I could see my blood seeping between the shards of glass like rose petals falling on ice.

As I walked, I secretly slipped my hand into my pocket and pressed the button on the telephone.

Varda's telephone, which was on the floor where it had fallen, began playing loud music. The same notes, over and over again.

Confused, Father Grigory swiveled his head around.

"What? Where—where is horrible music? Stop noise!"

I caught Varda's eye and winked. She understood that I had a plan. She winked back.

"It's nothing, just my telephone," Varda said to Father Grigory. "I'll shut it off. Just let me bend to get it."

"Da!" he said. "But make quick!"

Father Grigory loosened his grip on Varda only enough so that she could pick up her telephone. I hoped that she knew what I wanted her to do: press the receive button.

"BldofZar," I typed on my telephone with my thumb, "on321."

I watched Varda's face as she glanced at her telephone. I could see her nod slightly, ever so slightly. She understood!

Gritting my teeth against the pain, I continued my unbearably painful journey across the floor of broken glass, counting backward from *desyat*. Now only a half-dozen feet separated me from Varda! Just *a few more steps*, and . . .

"Very good, little mule," Father Grigory said to me. "You are braver than I thought. But Father Grigory change mind." He ran his rough fingers slowly through Varda's hair as she cringed. "Seems such a waste to free pretty girl. I think I kill you—and keep her!"

Holy Mother, please let this work! I shut my eyes and pictured in my mind the red river of time—flowing backward.

"Three . . . two . . . one," I said soundlessly, my lips barely moving. I knew that Varda could see my face on her telephone screen. Quickly, I reached out my hand to her, and she grabbed it.

"Mother of God, Blood of the tsar, I have no fear, Now send me far!" we shouted together.

CHAPTER TWENTY-SIX

"MOVE ALONG THERE. STAY IN LINE!"

"Ow!"

A man wearing a strange uniform pushed me with the butt of his rifle. The red river I'd pictured in my mind seconds before was replaced by something real: the red flag he carried on a pole. Varda and I found ourselves outdoors, at the end of a long line of peasants.

"Leave him alone!" Varda said to the man, who scowled at her.

"They say that even their toilet seats are made of gold!" a woman wearing a babushka said to the old lady standing next to her in line.

"Where are we?" Varda asked me.

I looked around, hardly daring to believe my eyes.

"Home. Tsarskoye Selo."

"Then why are all these people here?"

"I—I don't know," I said.

"Alexei—your voice! It's changing!"

"What?"

She was right. I could hear my voice crack, then get lower. A cool breeze suddenly brushed my wrists. My shirt cuffs were moving up my arms!

"Your arms!" Varda said. "They're growing!"

Once again, she was right. I watched in horror as my white sticklike arms appeared before my eyes in the bright summer sun. My legs felt strange, and then I looked down to find my ankles showing, as my pants grew shorter on my legs. And the glass cuts and blood on my feet disappeared before my very eyes!

"Alexei!" Varda said, staring at me like she had just seen the ghost of Ivan the Terrible. "I—I don't think you're twelve years old anymore."

I nodded, too afraid to hear the sound of my own new deep voice. At last I cleared my throat and spoke again.

"How—how old do I look?"

She looked me over, turning me around.

"I don't know. At least thirteen, I guess. Maybe fourteen. You look like the boys whose bar mitzvahs I've gone to."

"Varda, what is happening to me?"

"I don't know. But my guess is we must have returned to Russia about a couple of years after you left! So that's why you're older."

"Varda, this—this is terrible!"

"Well, it's not so bad, really," she said, eyeing me in a strange new way. "I mean, you're kind of a hunk . . ."

"*Nyet*, I mean—what if we are too late to save them? What if my family is already dead? Varda, show me your book."

"Book? What book?"

"Your book, your *book*! Russian history."

"I—I left it at home."

"What? We need book!"

"Well, it's not like I'm a mind reader, you know! You didn't tell me to take it—and you only gave me about three seconds' notice before we did the time travel mumbo jumbo, remember?"

"Without book how will we know when my family is killed, where, by who—how they were taken? We will never find them in time!"

"Look, don't get all Russian gloomy on me, okay? We're not beat yet. Maybe it's not too late. Hey, wait a minute! How come if it's 1918 and you're older now, I'm not, like, minus seventy-seven?"

"When I left home to go to 2010, I stay same age I was when left Russia—as long as I return to same year. When you leave home in 2010, you stay same age you were then. Da?"

She shrugged. "Makes sense."

"Tickets! Where's your tickets?" the man in the uniform barked at us. The line had moved up and we now stood before the door to the palace.

"What tickets?" I said.

"What did that bozo say?" Varda asked. I translated for her.

"What did she say?" the man asked me, a suspicious glint in his eye.

"She said, 'What did nice man say?'"

"Never mind, you!" the man said, pushing us along. "Keep moving!"

The rooms of the palace were filled with people. But I recognized no one. I smelled the familiar odor of rose oil from our icon lamps—but the icons and lamps were gone! The walls were stripped of their tapestries and paintings, our books were packed up in open boxes. *Where are the servants? Where is my family?*

A group of several dozen ragged children entered the room.

"Orphans, all orphans, line up over here! Boys on left, girls on right!" a woman announced. The children lined up in two rows in front of her. "You'll be living in the royal children's rooms. Upstairs, now—double time!"

What?

A very heavy peasant woman wearing dirty clothes sat right down on my favorite chair, which had a big white tag attached to it that read Tsarskoye Selo, rocking chair, item #4763. "Look at me! I'm the tsarina!" she said, putting a round bialy roll on her head like a crown and rocking faster and faster. *CRACK!* My chair split in two, and the woman tumbled to the floor with a *thump!*

A man picked up a book and read the inscription mockingly to his wife, who was standing next to him.

"'For my darling Alix Xmas 1912 fr. Nicky.' How *charming....*"

"Give that to me!" I snatched the *Rubaiyat of Omar Khayyam* from him. He snatched the book right back. "Take your dirty hands off that!" I said. "It's mine!"

"Oh, it's yours, is it, comrade? And who appointed you tsar?"

I grabbed for the book again, and we each pulled on it furiously in a tug-of-war.

"There, now! Are you satisfied?" he said. "Look what you've done!" The book had torn in two.

I wept bitterly. Varda put a comforting hand on my shoulder.

A guard walked into the room. He spat on the parquet floor.

"What's going on here?"

"This boy! He has desecrated state property!"

The man showed the guard the two halves of the torn book.

The guard grabbed me by the collar.

"This is a museum, not a school yard for brawling!"

"*Museum?*"

"Get out!"

The guard yanked me with one hand, and Varda with the other, tossing us out the door.

CHAPTER TWENTY-SEVEN

"WHAT HAVE THEY DONE WITH MY FAMILY?"

Varda and I paced Alexander Park at Tsarskoye Selo, trying to think what to do next.

"Varda, you must remember! What did your history teacher say about murders?"

Her face scrunched up as if she were trying very hard to remember.

"All I know is that he said the tsar and his family were assassinated by the Bolsheviks. In the summer of 1918."

"Well, is summer now—we find out year! What *date* in summer was family killed? Where? Please, Varda, *think*!"

"I told you—I don't know!"

Varda turned away—bumping right into a pretty young woman who was carrying a big basket containing bundles tied with string. The basket tumbled from the woman's hands, and she fell in a heap on the grass.

"Idiot!"—or worse—she seemed to mutter in a language (Yiddish?) that I didn't understand.

"I'm so sorry!" Varda said, helping her up. Varda stooped to pick up the bundles while the woman talked to herself angrily.

"Alexei!" Varda said, waving a bundle at me. "Look! She has newspapers!"

"Excuse me, miss," Varda said, using her hands to act out her words. "Can I borrow your newspaper?"

The woman scowled, waiting in vain for a kopeck. Then she reluctantly handed Varda a paper.

I read the headline—TROTSKY'S RED ARMY BEATS BACK WHITE GUARD—and the date.

"July 10, 1918! This is *Pravda*—revolutionary worker's newspaper," I said to Varda. "Papa shut down this paper years ago. Is back! This mean Bolsheviks already in charge of country!"

"Are you sure?"

"Da! Mother of God! They are worst of worst!"

"Don't panic, maybe it's not too late! Hey! Maybe this lady knows something. Ask her what they did with the royal family!"

I asked the young woman if she could speak Russian. She replied "Da," so I asked her Varda's question.

"*Abdicated!*" I said in Russian after listening to her long reply. The woman nodded vigorously.

I turned to Varda. "Papa must have been forced! He would never abandon Mother Russia!"

"Forced to do what?" Varda said anxiously. "What's

she saying?"

I motioned for Varda to be silent, then turned back to the young woman.

"Did no one try to save the Romanovs?"

"*Nyet!*" she said, and continued to explain, waving her hands and talking rapidly.

"Alexei—for God's sake, tell me what she's saying!"

"She says that after tsar abdicate last year, new government hold royal family under house arrest here for months. Then last summer local peasants spot some men putting tsar and tsarina and their girls on train with traveling bags. Peasants did not see the heir. She says family look very sad. This is all she knows."

Suddenly the woman stepped closer to Varda and me—eyeing our clothing curiously. Fortunately, till now nobody seemed to notice how strangely we were dressed; the peasants wore badly matched clothing themselves, and were too busy with their own problems to study ours. But then the woman put her nose close to mine and inspected my face. I felt a trickle of cold sweat run down my cheek.

"We have met before, da?" she said, looking at me with suspicion. "What is your name, comrade?"

I prayed that she didn't recognize me from pictures as the tsar's son.

"Uh . . . Lance," I replied. "Lance Armstrongovich. What is yours?"

"Tillie Spivack," she said.

"Tillie Spivack!" Varda said, grabbing my shirt

sleeve. "Ask her if she's a Russian Jew from Omsk and has a son named Josef. Tell her I am a friend, and not to be afraid."

I asked the woman Varda's question.

"Da!" she replied.

"Alexei!" Varda said, tugging my sleeve. "This woman—she's my great-great grandmother! The one in that photo I showed you!"

"Is so?"

"*That's* why we ended up here—the river of time brought us right to one of my relatives!"

"Now I know where Varda got bad temper!"

"Very funny. Wow, this is way cool. Look, I want to hang out with Tillie for a while."

"Varda, my family is in danger. We must go! We travel to Petrograd. Maybe we find out more there," I said, starting to walk away.

"Just give me a few minutes with my *bubbe*!"

"Your what?"

"That's Yiddish for 'grandma.' I know some Yiddish; I bet she speaks it—all the Russian Jews did. I want to talk with her."

"No! We leave now!"

Varda frowned, sighed, and followed me.

"Tyrant," she said, kicking the dirt with her feet as she walked.

Varda's great-great-grandmother had already wandered off, busy handing out newspapers in exchange for kopecks.

As we crossed Alexander Park to get to the train station, we passed a tree. I stuck my hand in the knothole.

"What are you doing?" Varda asked.

I pulled a small book—*this* book—out of the tree.

"Story of Alexei's life. *The Curse of the Romanovs*," I said. "Book I am writing."

"Why do you keep it in a tree?"

"So secret police won't find. So nosy sisters won't find."

I remembered the last thing I wrote before I went to the future. It was the beginning of Chapter 11, when I asked Gilliard to take me to Petrograd to see Cousin Felix.

"Can I read it?" Varda asked me.

"Someday . . . maybe," I said.

I put the book in my front pocket. *I swear by the Holy Mother, while I live, it shall never again leave my side!*

I would catch up on writing my story at every possible moment. I would have to write much faster now—not knowing what my *sudba* might be.

I showed Varda a letter carved into the tree bark.

"See this?" She nodded. "That is where my grandpa Sasha carved his initial, long time ago. This is how I make sure find right tree where book is."

"Why are you writing a book?"

"Many people tell lies about my family! Alexei Nikolaevich does not tell lies."

CHAPTER TWENTY-EIGHT

WE STOLE A RIDE TO PETROGRAD

in the back of a peasant's wagon—hiding under sacks filled with duck down. The feathers made such a cozy bed that I soon drifted off to sleep. I was very weary, and don't know how long I slept.

"Alexei!" Varda whispered, rudely nudging me from tender dreams of *Prianik medoviy* (honey cakes). "I think we're here."

The wagon had come to a stop. Petrograd! We hopped off and dashed away before the driver could catch a glimpse of us.

The first thing I noticed in Petrograd was something quite amazing: The sky was blue. Now, you may not think this a very strange thing. But the smoke from our factories used to make the skies always gray here. I guessed that the factories must not be so busy anymore.

The streets had very few people on them compared

to the Petrograd I remembered. Many of the people were very thin and coughing, or otherwise looked ill. And everywhere there were big ugly machine guns, with soldiers behind them eyeing everyone with suspicion.

A group of unshaven men wearing drab tunics and carrying rifles on their shoulders marched down the street at a goose step. They were headed straight for us!

"Come quickly!" I said, grabbing Varda by the arm. "Through alley!"

Breathless, we hid behind some waste cans at the side of a building. *Stomp-stomp-stomp!* The soldiers passed by us so closely that I could smell the sweat of a thousand forced marches. I couldn't resist taking a quick peek at them. *Ah! So these pitiful-looking specimens are the fearsome Red Army of the Bolsheviks! Not at all the spit-and-polish soldiers of Papa's Imperial Guard!*

I squinted against the bright sunlight reflecting off the shiny bayonets on their Mosin-Nagant rifles. Then I watched the regiment march out of view.

Varda and I stayed hidden until the rhythmic beat of the soldiers' boots faded to nothing and we were sure we were not being followed.

On the brick wall of the building, old posters with my papa's handsome face on them hung by a thread, in tatters. Pasted up in their place were other posters. One showed a man waving his fist and shouting—

with the caption: COMRADE LENIN LEADS US TO ULTIMATE VICTORY! He had a pointy beard, like the devil, and a lot of hair under his nose—but very little on top of his head. I could tell I would not like this Mr. Lenin.

Another poster showed the tsar, a priest, and a rich man "on the shoulders of the laboring people," crushing and whipping them. What lies! FOR THE RED ARMY, THERE ARE NO OBSTACLES! another illustration proclaimed, as a line of soldiers snaked up the mountains toward a brilliant sun. One poster had a woman on it carrying a basket of food on her shoulders. It said WOMEN, GO INTO COOPERATIVES!

"Look! Shoes!" Varda said, handing me a discarded pair of men's boots she'd found in the waste can. They had holes but fit me not too badly.

As Varda and I rounded the bend of the alley, we saw a bent old woman waving a heavy cane and cornering a big bony rat in an alley.

"Come here, *lyubimaya*, come to mama," she said.

It hissed at her. She hit the rat many times. With a final hiss, like the air going out of a bicycle tire, the rat was silent. Then she picked it up by its pink tail, letting it spin in circles as she studied it with appreciation. The woman licked her thin lips.

We watched, mouths dropped open in fascinated horror.

"Keep away from me!" she snarled, swinging her cane wildly at us. "Go find your own supper!"

We backed away from her, then ran across the street. Pausing to catch our breath, we sat down on the stairs of the Smolny Institute, a school for young noble girls.

"Do you know anyone in Petrograd who might be able to help us?" Varda asked me. "Someone who might know where your family was taken?"

I shook my head, then suddenly remembered: "Wait! *Do* know someone! Someone . . . wonderful!"

CHAPTER TWENTY-NINE

"YOU'LL FIND HIM IN THERE," SAID A STAGEHAND, pointing to a side entrance of the building. "Poor devil," he muttered mysteriously, shaking his head.

We entered and walked to the back of the empty theater.

Onstage, completely alone, was Vaslav Nijinsky—dancing like a man possessed, to music that only he could hear. He danced across the empty stage of the Mariinsky with a strange and jerky motion, as if pulled by invisible strings. This was a role I'd seen him dance before: Petrouchka, the lovesick wooden puppet who was hacked to pieces by his rival, the Moor, only to rise and dance again. But now Nijinksy moved as if he did not care whether he danced himself to death. Sweat poured in rivers down his bare arms and chest, his feet bled. His eyes looked dark and hollow; I could count his ribs.

Nijinsky had not seen us come in. He suddenly stopped, turned to his right, listening—as if he'd heard someone speak to him from the audience. He addressed a row of empty seats.

"I showed my wife the blood on my feet. She does not like blood. I told her that blood was war and I do not like war."

He cocked his ear and listened again—to no one.

"You are wrong! My wife, she love me very much! She is just afraid for me because I played nervously today. Come closer—I tell you secret. . . ." He leaned forward as if whispering in someone's ear. "I played nervously because the audience will understand me better if I am nervous. I was nervous because God wanted to arouse the audience. The audience came to be amused. They thought Nijinsky dance to amuse them! Ha! I dance frightening things. They are frightened of me and think that I want to kill them. I do not want to kill anyone. I love everyone, but no one loves me!"

He tore at his hair, and sat down on the wooden floor, face in his hands.

"Alexei," Varda whispered nervously in my ear. "He's just acting—*isn't he*?"

"I—I don't think so," I whispered back.

Nijinsky suddenly looked up and noticed us.

"And you!" he said, pointing to us with a shaky finger. "You are worst of all!"

"Is me, Vaslav. Alexei. Alexei Romanov, the tsarevich. Remember?"

"Why do you laugh at Nijinsky!"

"I—I did not laugh."

"The audience started laughing! I started laughing. I laughed at my dance. The audience understood my dance, for they wanted to dance too. I danced badly because I kept falling on floor when did not have to. The audience not care because I dance beautifully. They understood my tricks and enjoy themselves! I wanted to dance more, but God say to me: 'Enough!' I stopped."

Suddenly he leaped up, his head snapping toward the wings.

"He comes for me!"

We looked where he was looking, but saw or heard no one. "Who—who is coming for you?"

"The Moor! He will stop at nothing to kill Petrouchka! Quick—we must hide!"

He crouched down on the stage, curling up into a ball, his hands over his head. He trembled, and we could hear the sound of quiet weeping.

We climbed the stairs to the stage.

"Please, do not be afraid, Vaslav!" I patted him gently on the back, but he cringed. "I have slain the Moor with my sword," I said soothingly. "You see? He is gone. He will not bother you anymore."

Slowly, Nijinsky raised his head to look up at me, like a turtle coming out of his shell.

I nodded to him, and saw the trace of a childlike smile forming through his tears.

Varda tugged at my sleeve and whispered.

"Alexei, I think we should go."

CHAPTER THIRTY

"HOW SAD! WAS HE ALWAYS LIKE THAT?" Varda said as we walked out into the hallway.

"*Nyet, nyet*—of course not. War does strange things to people, Papa says. Nijinksy is sensitive artist, maybe war, all this, too much for him."

We passed by the open door to a storage closet.

"Look!" Varda said. "Theater costumes!"

She started rummaging through the boxes.

"Varda! We must go—no time to play dress-up!"

"Wait a minute!" she said. "This is important! The Bolsheviks have got your family. They must be out looking for you under every cabbage leaf. Right?"

"Da. Suppose so."

"You're Russia's most wanted man! Maybe most of the peasants don't know what you look like. But I bet the Bolsheviks do. They must have sent out an Amber Alert on you."

"Sent *what*?"

"Look, you can't keep walking around looking like you. Sooner or later somebody's going to recognize you and rat you out. My teacher said Lenin snuck back into Russia disguised in a red wig and took over the whole country. If he got away with it, maybe you can too!"

She reached into a box and took out a costume.

"Here," she said, "try this on for size."

"*Nyet!* Will not wear woman's dress!"

"Picky, picky! Here. How about this?"

We put a peasant's cap and jacket on me, along with a beard. I looked at myself in a mirror on the wall.

"Beard itches."

"You look like Harvey Fierstein in *Fiddler on the Roof*," she said, "but it'll have to do."

Varda took a shawl to cover her own clothing, and we went outside.

"What time is it? I'm hungry," Varda said.

I looked at the sky, then at the street.

"Probably near eleven at night. All shops been closed many hours."

"That's impossible! It's still light outside."

"*Beliye Noche.*"

"What?"

"White nights. We are far north here, sun never set in Petrograd during a few days in summer."

"Wow! And they call *New York* 'the city that never sleeps'!"

Suddenly I felt a rough push from behind.

"*Stoi!*"

We halted—and looked behind us to find two Red Army soldiers, rifles pressed firmly into our backs.

"Who are your people, comrade?" the sergeant said to me in Russian.

"Peasant farmers. From the east."

The man looked at me suspiciously.

"Pah! You talk too good for a peasant. What crop you grow?"

"Uh . . . I—"

"I thought so. Liar! What about girl?"

Varda opened her mouth, but I jumped in before she could say anything.

"Mute. The tsar's secret police cut out her tongue."

The sergeant nudged the corporal next to him.

"Good thing for a woman not to speak, eh, Krepinsky?"

They slapped each other on the back, laughing till their rotten teeth showed.

The sergeant's face turned sour again. He stepped around to the front of us and stared at my shirt, whose lettering peeked out from under my peasant jacket. He yanked my jacket rudely aside for a closer look.

"What mean this word? Foreign, anti-Bolshevik propaganda?"

"*Nyet!*" I said. "'Livestrong.' It mean . . . 'Long Live Lenin!'"

"You think quickly, *mouzhik*." He poked me in the

chest with his finger. "Not much meat on his bones, eh, Krepinsky? But smart in the head. Come along!"

He and the other man nudged me forward with the rifle.

"Wait! Where are we going?

"Red Army can use smart *mouzhik*."

He pushed me onto the back of a run-down truck.

"Red Army? But—"

"Alexei!" Varda screamed, running toward us.

"Hey!" Krepinsky said. "Thought you said she couldn't talk?"

The soldiers hopped into the cab of the truck, slamming the doors behind them.

"Alexei! Where are they taking you?"

Varda ran after us as fast as she could. But it was too late.

The truck—with me in it—had already pulled away.

CHAPTER THIRTY-ONE

"ODIN, DVA, TRI, CHETYRE!

Odin, dva, tri, chetyre!"

A soldier was drilling Red Army troops at their camp near the railroad tracks just outside Petrograd. He slapped his arm sharply against his leg with each count, demanding that they march to his beat.

An armored train pulled into the station, and a man in an army greatcoat strode down the stairs with a self-important air. He was immediately surrounded by officers who stepped all over one another trying to please him.

The man ignored them, instead studying the drilling exercise at camp with a critical eye, his dark mustache twitching with impatience. He took out his monacle, polished it quickly on his handkerchief, then squinted it back into his eye socket.

The sergeant and Krepinsky dragged me by the elbow, planting me in front of the man with the monacle. The sergeant "snapped to," saluting him.

"*Commisar!*" he announced. "I recruit this man, new volunteer, myself!"

Volunteer? Hah!

"Another little fish caught in the Neva, eh, Sergeant? You are dismissed!"

The sergeant and Krepinsky saluted again and marched away.

"I am Commisar Trotsky," the officer said to me. "And you have the high honor of serving in the People's Army."

"I could have done without the honor, sir."

I immediately regretted my words. But to my surprise he smiled.

"So, you do not believe in our cause, comrade?"

As Gilliard says, you cannot unring a bell, so I forged ahead.

"Everyone wants the peasants and workers of Russia to have enough food to eat. Even the tsar. It just depends on how."

"The *ex*-tsar, you mean." *Ex? Was Papa already dead?* "The end may justify the means as long as there is something that justifies the end. When you are older, you will know. There are no absolute rules of conduct, either in peace or war. Everything depends on circumstances. Where are you from, young man?"

"New York, most recently."

"Ah! I was there myself, last year. Waiting for a more . . . comfortable climate in Russia. How are things in New York these days?"

"I—I don't think you would recognize it, sir."

"Hmm . . . yes, the world changes very fast now. I trust you will enjoy your stay with us. A young man needs time to think about his view of the world. Over there is the latrine. You will have plenty of time to think while you are cleaning it. You are dismissed!"

He strode quickly away.

"Here!" a soldier barked, handing me a smelly shovel. "Get busy!" I glanced up at him.

"Derevenko!"

It was one of my two *diadkas*!

I pulled down my beard a little so he could get a look at my face.

He stared at me, his mouth dropping open.

"Derevenko, did they kidnap you, too? Thank God you are all right! Where is my family?"

He ignored my question, then pointed to the toilet. "Clean that out!"

"What? It's me, Derevenko! Alexei! Don't you recognize me?"

"You heard me!" Then he spoke in a mocking voice. "'Move my leg, Derevenko,' 'Get me that book, Derevenko,' 'Hurry up, fatty—carry me over there!' For three hundred years you Romanovs told me and my family what to do. *I'm* giving the orders now!"

I was stunned by his words, and the cold hatred I saw in his eyes.

"Derevenko—please! I know you are angry. Maybe—

maybe I can even understand why. But you must help me!"

"*Help* you? You should count yourself lucky I don't turn you in!"

He shoved a bucket of soapy water into my hand and turned away. I ran after him.

"Please, I beg of you! Just tell me one thing! Where did they take my family?"

"So you beg, eh? Is nice to see you beg."

"I'm sorry if I was cruel to you! Really."

"Sorry? Sorry fixes nothing! I'll tell you where Bloody Nicholas is, and your German witch of a mother, too. They were taken to Tobolsk, may they rot in hell. There!"

I gathered up my courage to ask one more question.

"Are they—Did they kill them?"

But Derevenko had already walked away.

STATON RABIN

CHAPTER THIRTY-TWO

MOST OF THE SOLDIERS WERE SLEEPING under the midnight sun.

I stole some bread from the mess area. It was moldy but I was too hungry to care. Then I stayed up all night in the tent they had assigned to me, writing in my book.

If only I could find some way to escape and get to Tobolsk! But the guards kept a watchful eye. I prayed I was not already too late to save my family.

And what about Varda? A pretty young American girl alone in Petrograd, in the middle of famine and civil war! And with so many brutal, godless men roving about. I shuddered at the thought of what might happen to her!

I glanced over at my tent mate—a tired old man who seemed more ready for the rocking chair than the front lines of battle. The tent flaps fluttered with each blast from his snoring.

Suddenly the man bolted awake at a sound.

"What?" he sputtered. "Is it morning already?"

"No."

"Damn bugler, playing reveille in middle of night!"

But it wasn't the bugler. It was music from my little telephone!

"Uh . . . I'll see if I can get the bugler to be quiet," I told him, slipping out of the tent.

I hid behind a tree and pressed the telephone's on button.

"Alexei, thank God! Press the green button to talk."

"Varda!"

"I was *sure* our cell phones couldn't work here—no cell towers in 1918—so I didn't even try calling you. But then it just hit me: Varda, you idiot, these are those new combo cell phone–walkie-talkies! Where there's no cell service, they automatically switch over to their two-way radio frequencies. They don't need cell towers, as long as we're within a fifteen-mile radius of each other!"

"Huh?"

"Never mind that now. Where are you?"

"Am—with Red Army, about five versts outside Petrograd. Next to water tower and railroad tracks. Where are you?"

"With my bubbe Tillie. I looked all over for you, then hitched a ride back to Tsarskoye Selo with some singing Gypsies who speak a little Yiddish. Bubbe took me home and fed me. She's really nice when you get to know her. Makes a great—what did she call it?—borscht soup, too."

"My family—they are in Tobolsk!"

"Where is that?"

"Siberia. I hope I am not too late!"

"It's kind of cold there, isn't it?"

"Only some parts, not this time of year. We must go to Tobolsk!"

"All right, all right. Look, stay where you are. I'll find some way to get to you. I'll help you escape!"

"Da. Good."

"Alexei?"

"Da?"

"How far is a verst?"

CHAPTER THIRTY-THREE

I SLEPT FOR A FEW HOURS, then was awakened by music from my telephone. I went outside to answer it.

"I'm right outside your camp," Varda said on the screen. "I can see you. Tell me where the sentries are posted and how many."

I looked around and counted.

"*Tri* on north side, *odin* on east, and . . . *dva* on north and south."

"Only one sentry at the east?"

"Da," I said. "He's near water tower."

"Where? No—I see him! If you can get past him, you're free. I'm going to distract him."

"How?"

"Never mind that. The second you see him leave his post and go inside a tent, make a run for it. Be careful not to fall. I'll meet you behind the water tower. Get it?"

"Got it."

"Good."

I kept an eye on the sentry, using field glasses I'd found inside my tent. I hung the field glasses by their leather strap around my neck.

Soon I saw a woman in a red dress slink up to the sentry, swaying her hips like a *prostituka*. No, not "a" woman. Varda!

Zdorovo! Wow!

I saw the sentry take off his cap and smile at her. He kept nervously dropping his cap and picking it up! He spoke to her, but Varda didn't say anything back. No wonder! She didn't speak any Russian! But she spoke the only language every man can understand. Wiggling her hips, Varda touched his arm, then traced a finger across his lips. He nodded sheepishly. She pointed to a tent and gave him a little push, as if to say: *Go ahead. I will follow in a minute.*

The sentry glanced quickly from side to side, as if to make sure no one was watching him. Then he deserted his post and went inside the tent. *Brava, Varda!*

I ran as fast as I could to the water tower, where Varda was already waiting for me. We hugged like we hadn't seen each other in a hundred years.

We barely had time to congratulate ourselves before the sentry, pants down around his legs, came running furiously out of the tent, looking every which way. He spotted us! Shouting angry curses, he woke up half the Red Army.

"*Dezertir!*"

We took off running. In seconds a whole battalion was coming after us!

"Hurry, Alexei!"

We ran for our lives, but my bad legs slowed me down, and the soldiers were quickly gaining on us. They started firing shots in our direction.

"Get down!" she shouted.

"Look!" I said, pointing. A train came rumbling down the tracks toward us. "Jump on!"

"It's not going to stop! We can't; you'll get hurt!"

This was no time for arguments. I grabbed her hand.

"On three!" I said. "*Odin, dva, tri!*"

I leaped onto the train car—its door was slid back a few feet—pulling Varda up behind me. A soldier on the ground made a running grab at her ankle, and . . . *caught!*

I pulled and pulled, hanging on to Varda with all my strength, while the soldier, running to keep up, pulled her leg in the opposite direction. Then the train sped up, and we broke free, falling backward together into the train car—leaving the soldier and the Red Army far behind.

"*Spasibo* for breaking my fall," I said.

"Anytime, comrade," she said, rubbing her sore leg. "But next time I think I'd rather take my chances with the Red Army."

We turned around.

"Breakfast is served, madam!" I said, bowing like our footman, Trupp. We were in a car full of vegetables—at least a *tysyacha* kilos' worth.

Varda laughed.

The engineer must have left the door open by mistake—with so many starving Russians around, this cargo wouldn't last long.

We sat down, smashing open melons and stuffing tomatoes into our mouths till our faces were sticky with juice.

I stared at her, smiling.

"What are *you* looking at? Haven't you ever seen a girl pig out before?"

"Where did you get dress?" I asked her.

"From my bubbe—she gave me one of hers."

"Very nice."

"*Spasibo*," she said.

I suddenly felt shy, but I was determined to ask her my question.

"Varda, what happen if hemophiliac boy marry girl who is carrier?"

She made a choking noise and spit out some melon seeds.

"You mean like . . . you and me?"

"Da. And they have children someday."

"Alexei! We can't get married. Not that it's such a crazy idea . . . you're kind of cute. But, I mean, we're cousins! Like, that's illegal or something!"

"My mama and papa were *kuzin*, and they marry."

"That's different; they're royalty! Those people always marry their relatives."

"You are royalty too."

"Oh, yeah. That's right, I forgot. 'Princess Varda.' I like the sound of that." She leaned back against a huge pile of potatoes. "Well . . . let's see. If a hemophiliac male has kids with a female carrier, all their daughters would be carriers, and 50 percent of their children of either sex would have the disease."

"Oh," I said, disappointed. "But maybe they have cure by then! Maybe *you* find cure."

"Yes. That's certainly possible."

"So . . . You think Alexei is 'cute,' eh?"

She looked at me and tried to hide her smile.

"Well, don't be getting a swelled head or anything. But I think that on the cuteness scale, you'd rate about a *devyat*-and-a-half."

I leaned closer to her.

"*Devyat*-and-a-half. This is good?"

"Uh . . . very good," she said.

"Not full *desyat*?"

"All right. Maybe *desyat*."

And then I did something I had never done before in my life.

I kissed her.

CHAPTER THIRTY-FOUR

BOOM!

"'Was that cannon fire,'" Varda asked, breaking our kiss, "'or is it my heart pounding?' I always wanted to say that. . . ."

"Huh?"

"It's from an old movie, *Casabl*—Never mind."

"Is not guns, just thunder. Do not be afraid, Little Peasant. Just storm coming."

Together we slid the train doors all the way back and sat down to watch the storm. Lightning flashed jaggedly across the sky.

"Alexei, are you sure this train is going the right way to take us to Siberia?"

"Da," I said. "Is Trans-Siberian route. But only goes as far as Tyumen—that's nearest stop to Tobolsk. We take boat or horses from there."

"Do you think there are any other people on this train?"

"Engineer. Train cannot drive itself, da?"

"I mean *passengers*."

"Maybe," I said. "War trains carry soldiers, peasants, food, supplies—all on same train. Owners keep cargo secret from passengers."

"Let's look in the other cars. Maybe we can find someone who knows what happened to your family."

The rain was coming down like Noah's flood.

"Watch step! Take my hand," I told Varda, helping her pass between cars of the moving train. "Is slippery."

"Yes, Your Majesty," she said not quite seriously.

We entered the next car. Varda stood staring in amazement at what we found there.

"Jeez. This place has more guns than an NRA pep rally."

"Hmmm . . . *Eierhandgranate*," I said, inspecting the weapons.

"Huh?"

"Egg bombs, German hand grenades. You just pull pin, and—*Ka-boom!* Red Army must have captured these from enemy." I pointed to some big weapons on wheels. "Maxim Sokolov machine guns, old 1910 model. All steel, 7.62 × 54 mm R caliber, muzzle velocity eight hundred sixty meter per second."

"How do you know all that?"

"Will command Russian army someday. Is my job to know."

We passed into the next car, and found it crowded

with miserable-looking peasants and tired, dusty soldiers. Everyone smelled like old sweat and cheap wine.

"Excuse, please," I said, as we squeezed past a bunch of them. We were lucky to find a seat.

After a few minutes a smelly, ragged peddler, wearing a dark hood despite the warm weather, came down the aisle. He was carrying a box of goods on a strap that hung from his neck.

"Rags, sewing notions, sundries!" People scowled and shook their heads or ignored him.

He offered us his goods.

"*Nyet, spasibo*," I said.

"Ah, but insist take closer look at this," he said, removing an item from the box and holding it up for my examination. "Might find of particular interest . . ."

It was a knitting needle.

Mother of God! *Him!*

"Varda! Run!" I shouted, yanking her up by the sleeve.

We forced our way through the crowd and leaped into the gap between the moving train cars.

I took a quick glance behind us. Father Grigory was only steps behind—but his goods tray got stuck between the car doors. He was struggling to remove the strap from his neck to get free.

"Up there!" I shouted to Varda, pointing to the roof of the train. Rain pounded down in a steady stream, like machine gun bullets on metal. "Quick!"

"No way!"

I ignored her protests and dragged her up the rain-slick metal ladder after me.

"Alexei, you'll fall!"

We crawled onto the roof of the galloping train, clinging to it desperately like baby possums clutching the fur on their mother's back. Then we rose slowly to our feet like drunken sailors who can't get their sea legs. The train roared over the Ural Mountains, sending puffs of hot black smoke high into the air.

"Alyosha!" Father Grigory had scrambled up onto the roof after us! "In name of God, stop!"

He scrambled to his feet and barreled after us. Varda and I came to the edge of a five-foot gap between roofs of the moving cars.

I grabbed her hand. "Jump!"

But Varda stood frozen with fear.

Crack!

Lightning struck the train's first car just in front of us. There was nowhere left to run. *Trapped!*

"Do not fear," Father Grigory said, making the sign of the cross as he approached us. "I have come to help Alexei save his family."

"*What?*" Varda said.

"If Bolsheviks kill Romanovs, it is end of Mother Russia, end of church—end of all that is holy. Do you not see? We must help each other and save them."

"You tried to kill me!" I said.

"A thousand times I save your life. And, da, once in

anger I try to take it—after you and Felix try to take mine! Have you forgotten? I pray to Holy Mother to forgive you. I have forgive. Now I ask you to forgive me! For sake of your family, your country."

"Liar!" Varda said. "Don't believe him, Alexei!"

"Girl is wise," he replied. "Father Grigory not always to be trusted, da? But this you know is true: We need each other, Alyoshenka! And Mother Russia, she need us both—more than ever now."

I glanced at Varda, and saw in her eyes what she was about to do. She dashed behind Father Grigory and pushed him.

With a scream he slipped and fell between the cars. At the last second he grabbed onto one of them. Barely hanging on with one hand, he dangled only a few feet above the powerful rolling wheels of the speeding train.

Father Grigory made a desperate grab for the railing with his other hand, trying to pull himself up—but it was too far away. His muscles shook from the strain of hanging on; his eyes pleaded for my help. "You and I, one cannot exist without the other. Like bread needs salt." He stared at me, eyes boring into my soul. *And like son needs his father.*

His words hit me like a thunderbolt.

"Da, is true, Alexei. Did you never suspect it? Why you think I leave wife and family alone in Siberia to help sickly boy? How did tsar with nothing but daughters suddenly have son? From sorcerer's magic or miracle prayers to saints? Pah! Look into mirror, Alyoshenka. Look very hard. Eyes you will see looking back at you are mine."

Could it be? "You are my—"

Father Grigory nodded.

Suddenly everything I had seen between him and my mother, everything that had happened in my life, made perfect sense. Wherever I went—past, present, or future—*this* was why he was always able to find me. And, in truth, I had suspected it all along.

Father Grigory's strength gave out, he slipped farther toward the deadly rails. He made one last, desperate reach toward me.

It was as if Varda could read my mind.

"No, Alexei!" Varda shouted.

But I had made my decision. I grabbed Father Grigory's hand, and with the last *untsiya* of my strength and his, pulled him back to safety on the train.

"God bless you, my boy," he said, tears in his eyes. He kissed my hand, then put it to his chest. "When Alexei bleeds, Grigory bleeds. When Alexei suffers, Grigory suffers too. This is how God made it, and how will always be. As long as my strong blood runs in your fragile veins, and your warm heart beats in mine."

Could he be trusted? Somehow I knew that in this, at least, he could.

But whatever the truth about the circumstances of my birth, I was still the tsarevich. And my mother, sisters, and the tsar—the good man who'd raised me—were still the family that I loved. I owed them everything. And I would do anything in my power—anything!—to save them.

"Father, do you know where they've taken my family in Tobolsk?"

"They are in Tobolsk no more," Father Grigory said. "Am told Bolsheviks move them to Ekaterinburg here in Ural Mountains last May."

Varda asked the question I was afraid to ask myself.

"Are they still alive?"

"Da! For now. But who knows what godless Ural Soviet will do to them. There is not much time!"

"How far are we from Ekaterinburg?" Varda asked me.

"We are in luck," I said, peeking at her watch. "Next train stop." She looked impressed at my ready answer, but I pretended humility and shrugged. "Tsarevich knows railroad time tables in Russia like babies know mother's breast."

We climbed back down the ladder and found a seat inside the train compartment.

Two soldiers were staring at us. I suddenly realized my fake beard was hanging half off my face! I struggled to put it back on, but it wouldn't stick. Then one of the soldiers took a piece of paper out of his pocket that had a photograph on it, and showed it to the other man. They both pointed at us.

"The heir!"

Every head snapped toward me. Father Grigory grabbed my hand, and I grabbed Varda's. We bolted for the door, knocking over people in our path, as the train wound its way around the mountaintop.

"*Stoi!*" one of the soldiers shouted. But we kept on running.

He raised his Mauser at me and took careful aim.

"Don't shoot him!" the other soldier warned, knocking his rifle aside.

"Out of my way!" the other man said, taking aim again. "He's worth a million rubles alive or dead!"

Thinking quickly, Varda pulled the train's emergency brake. The train screeched to a violent halt, throwing soldiers and passengers forward on top of each other like a pile of herring.

Father Grigory and I scrambled to our feet and looked out the window. We were thousands of feet up, on the edge of a cliff. But there was a drop of only about ten feet to a narrow rocky ledge.

"You jump, I catch!" he whispered to Varda and me, pulling us by the hands. "Is only hope!"

Father Grigory ran to the front of the car, mumbled a prayer, then leaped out of the train, landing on the narrow ledge. Then he held out his arms to us. Varda went first, then me. He caught both of us, one at a time, in his strong peasant's arms. The ledge was barely wide enough to hold the three of us.

Several shots rang out.

"Alexei!"

Father Grigory jumped in front of me, shielding me from the bullets with his body. A half-dozen soldiers in the front car were breaking train windows with their rifle butts, then firing down at us like shooting mechanical rabbits in a carnival gallery.

I pushed Varda farther back on the ledge, so they could not get a good bead on her.

"A cigar to the first man who shoots the heir!" one soldier shouted to the others.

The bullets came at us like a swarm of bees, but it was hard for the soldiers to see us through the driving rain.

Suddenly, Father Grigory's body jerked like Petrouchka. He was hit! His face turned deathly pale, eyes rolling back in his head.

"*Do svidaniya*, my son," he whispered with his final breath. "Do not fear—God is with you!"

Father! Do not leave me!

I reached for his hand, but it was too late. Our Friend made the sign of the cross, then tumbled over the side of the rain-swept cliff, to meet his final *sudba*—alone.

CHAPTER THIRTY-FIVE

CRACK!

A bolt of lightning struck a huge pine tree twenty feet from us on the cliff above. Then we heard a sound like the shrieks of the damned in hell.

"Alexei, what's happening?"

"The tree! It's going to fall!"

"Which way?"

"Duck and pray!"

We crouched down on the rocky ledge, hands over our heads, preparing for the worst.

A few seconds later we heard a terrible crash.

All was silent like the tombs of my ancestors, then we heard screams and moans of pain. We looked up—the tree had missed us but landed right on the roof of the train, crushing it like a caviar tin.

I looked for a foothold to scramble back up from the ledge.

"Where are you going?" Varda said.

"People injured, they need help."

"Alexei, those people want to kill you!"

"Not all. Some are innocent! I help them, like Grandpa Sasha did in train crash at Borki."

She grabbed me by my jacket sleeve.

"Alexei, for God's sake, listen to me! There's nothing you can do for those people now. We have no bandages, no plasma. And if you go back in there, they'll shoot you—or take you prisoner! How will you be able to help your family then?"

But I would not listen to her. I scrambled back up the cliff, slip-sliding all the way, and Varda followed, still trying to stop me.

The train was lying on its side, derailed by the impact of the gigantic tree. I inspected the wreck.

"Alexei—be careful!"

I stepped carefully over the tree trunk and jagged, smoking mass of train metal. We peered into one of the train windows. It was a terrible scene. The soldiers who had been firing at us from the front car lay over the floor and crushed seats—dead.

We entered another one of the train cars, to a chorus of moans of pain.

One old peasant woman on the floor slowly raised her bloody head, staring at me in amazement.

"The tsarevich! Our angel sent from heaven!"

So! Not everyone in Russia is loyal to the Bolshevik cause!

"Are you all right, Mother?" I said to her, checking her forehead and helping her to her feet. I always call old ladies "Mother," as a sign of respect.

Varda and I went around to each of the passengers, to see if there was anything we could do to ease their suffering. In this car most of the people weren't seriously hurt, thank God. We tore up their shirts to wrap wounds, just as I'd seen my mother, Olga, and Tatiana do with real bandages at our army hospitals. We offered the passengers sips of water from dead soldiers' canteens.

As we got ready to leave them, promising to send help, the most amazing thing happened. Wounded or not, every passenger in the car rose slowly to his feet.

And they bowed to me.

We made our way gingerly down to the bottom of the deep canyon, where we found Father Grigory's body. By the grace of God, his hands were crossed neatly over his body, eyes staring up toward heaven, like a painting of a dead saint. The mist had cleared, and the rain clouds parted. Taking off my cap, I knelt and recited the Orthodox prayer for the dead that I'd heard the Metropolitan say in church so many times:

"Give rest, Lord, to the soul of your servant Father Grigory who has fallen asleep, in your kingdom, where there is no pain, sorrow, or suffering. In your goodness and love for all men, pardon all the sins he has committed in thought, word, or deed, for there is no man or woman who lives and sins not, you only are without sin."

I kissed Father Grigory's forehead.

We had no shovel to bury him, so Varda and I covered him with pine tree branches.

As we went on our way in the direction of Ekaterinburg, I kept looking back to the place where Father Grigory lay. He had survived so much before, part of me expected him to simply get up and fly away. But he was a man, not an angel, and men don't have wings.

After we'd walked a verst or two, Varda noticed I was limping.

"You bumped yourself," she said.

"*Nyet*," I said.

"Don't lie to me! You're hurt!"

"Is nothing. We must—we must get to Ekaterinburg."

But the pain was too great; I could not hide it from her any longer. I had bumped my ankle during the chase on the train.

I stumbled and fell.

"Alexei!"

She ran to my side, breaking my fall just in time.

"We must go," I said, struggling to get on my feet. "My family . . ."

"You're not going anywhere, Your Highness," she said, pushing me gently back down and examining my leg. "Not on that ankle." Varda propped my leg up on a rock, giving me water from the soldiers' canteens we'd brought with us from the train. She packed my ankle in mud, but it did about as little good as Dr. Botkin's mud treatments at home.

"What about pill?" I said.

"What pill?"

"Pill you make, show me in New York. 'Jeans therapy.'"

"*Gene* therapy. I don't have it with me, it's at home. Besides, that treatment hasn't been tested on people yet. It might kill you!"

"Okay," I said.

"Look, we can go back to my time. For factor VIII. Please, Alexei, let's go back to New York. The doctors there can help you!"

"*Nyet!* Must save my family!"

Within a few hours tears ran down my cheeks. I chewed my lips raw, trying to hold back the pain.

"Don't try to hold it in!" Varda said. "Don't be brave. You'll go crazy! *Do* something. Scream!"

"My family never let me scream at palace," I told her. "Afraid someone hear me."

"Well, scream all you want out here. No one will hear you. God knows, you've earned it."

I took a deep breath. "It hurts!" I yelled.

"Louder!" she said.

"It hurts!!!"

"*Louder!!*"

I screamed from the bottom of my toes, from the bottom of my soul. A whole lifetime of screams unscreamed.

STATON RABIN

My screams echoed off the mountaintops. "IT HURTS! HURTS! HURTS! HURTS!"

Varda was desperate to help me, but other than holding my hand, there was little she could do.

She felt my forehead.

"God, Alexei, you're burning up," she said.

"I need Father Grigory!"

"You can get well on your own. You've got to!"

"*Nyet!* He heals me. Alone, I die!"

"You're not alone. You've got me. You've got *you*. Think of your parents, your sisters. They need you. *I* need you. Please, Alexei, don't give up!"

But I grew weaker, and my eyes fluttered closed.

In my mind, I stood alone, up to my knees in a flowing river of blood, inside the narrow, winding blue tunnel of my veins. I listened to the ever-fainter beating of my heart. In my right hand I held a small gardener's shovel, and I was surrounded by buckets of soft, wet yellow sand, like the sand from the skerries. Suddenly a great rushing sound roared in my ears, as if a giant wave were barreling toward me. I heard it but could not see it. Working feverishly, desperately with my trowel, I built a dam of yellow sand against it. Then a massive wall of red liquid roared toward me like an onrushing train. As I drifted into unconsciousness, my last thought was: *Mother of God, I cannot fail my family! Please give me the strength.*

CHAPTER THIRTY-SIX

A FEW HOURS MUST HAVE PASSED. Many times I slipped in and out of awareness, hovering between this world and the next. When I finally awoke, Varda was sleeping, her head resting against a rock. I shook her.

"Wake up, Little Peasant!"

"What? What is it?" she said groggily, looking up at me. "Hey! You're *standing*!"

All my life, I had thought that it was Father Grigory's visits that had made me well. I'd look inside myself when I was ill, and find nothing of any use to me. But when I'd looked inside myself earlier that day, certain I'd reached the end of my strength, I looked harder—and found more. And when even this determination was gone, I reached deeper—and found *more*. My strength was like Anastasia's *matryoshka* doll: open it up, and inside there's another. Open that one, and there's another, and another.

In my mind I had imagined myself building a dam against the great wave of blood that had come crashing over me—and the dam had held!

Still, I knew that my strength and imagination alone could not explain how I had survived that day. Father Grigory could heal himself, as he had when that crazy woman had stabbed him in Siberia. Perhaps he had passed *some small portion* of this gift down to me through his blood—as surely as he had given me the color of my eyes. And perhaps, at least in this way, I was truly my father's son.

"I told you you could do it!" Varda said, standing now right beside me. She felt my forehead. "Your fever's gone. Can you walk?"

I leaned on her shoulder at first, but was able to walk much better as we went along. By the time the sun was directly overhead, I could manage well enough without assistance, and we had come many versts.

"Look!" Varda said, pointing. "There's a church steeple. A town!"

"Ascension Cathedral," I said. "It's Ekaterinburg!"

But off in the distance there was a faint thudding noise—and then we saw smoke, perhaps fifty versts from the other side of town.

"What's that?" Varda asked me.

"Artillery fire. Anti-Bolshevik White Army must be getting closer."

"That's good, isn't it? Maybe they'll reach Ekaterinburg and free your family."

"*Nyet, not* good," I said, shaking my head. "If Bolsheviks think White Army arrive soon, they will kill my family so can't be rescued."

We entered Ekaterinburg and came to a large building on the corner of Voznesensky Prospekt: Hotel Amerika.

"Let's try there, " Varda said. "A lot of people come through hotels. Maybe somebody knows where in Ekaterinburg your family is being held."

"Da," I replied. "But must be very careful how ask questions. We do not know which side of civil war these *mouzhiks* are on."

The man at the hotel's front desk was watering potted plants, polishing brass desk lamps, and sorting letters into little pigeonholes—all at the same time. His sweat made small oily pools on the desk, and his hands shook so much he knocked a plant over.

Without turning around, he seemed to sense we were standing there.

"What is it! Can't you see I'm busy?"

Muttering to himself, the man used a newspaper to sweep spilled dirt from the desk into a little trash can.

"We were wondering—"

The telephone rang. The man picked it up.

"Privet, Hotel Amerika," he answered the telephone, sounding bored and annoyed. He listened to the voice on the other end for a few seconds, then suddenly snapped to attention.

"Oh, it's *you*, Comrade Beloborodov!" he said nervously. "How nice to hear from you! . . . Da, everything is under control. Two o'clock sharp, lunch for twelve, room 3, it's all confirmed—Absolutely! . . . Change the reservation to one o'clock? As you wish, no problem at all. We have the finest chef in Ekaterinburg—only the best for the Ural Soviet!" *The local Bolshevik leaders! Coming here!* ". . . Da, comrade, I understand. Do not worry. You have my word that all will be ready in time for your arrival."

He rang a little bell on the desk and two maids—identical twins wearing sparkling white aprons and black bows in their hair, like toy terriers—appeared within seconds.

"I want room 3 spotless in fifteen minutes," the man commanded the maids.

"But our mother is home sick, and you gave us permission to leave by twelve thirty to care for her!"

"Well, I change my mind!" their boss replied. "Do what I say or you're both out of a job!"

Looking frightened, they nodded in unison, then trotted off.

"Now, what do *you* want?" the man at the desk asked us.

"Uh . . . There's been a train crash on the Trans-Siberian route a few miles north of town. Many people are hurt. Will you send help?" I said.

"Train crash! *Bozhe moj!* Just what I need on a day like this! All right," he said, scowling and picking up the phone again to dial a number. "I'll notify the Red Cross."

"We'll come back again when you're not so busy."

Varda whispered in my ear. "Did you ask him about your family?"

"*Nyet*, he can't be trusted. I have better idea. Come with me."

I followed the maids, and Varda followed me.

"Excuse please," I said to the maid on my left. "We have much experience cleaning very fussy rich man's home before revolution."

"Really? Who?"

"The tsar himself!"

The women crossed themselves, then looked at each other.

"The tsar!"

"Yes, he had very messy children. We'd be happy to clean that room for you while you go home to take care of your mother. We wouldn't want to see you get in trouble."

She grasped my hand.

"Would you? *Spasibo!* You're a godsend! It's room 3."

She opened the door for us with her key.

"Here are the cleaning supplies. Just polish the table, sweep the rug, clean the windows, and set out the silverware and glasses. The food is already in there."

"Alexei!" Varda said, taking the rags I handed her and eyeing me suspiciously. "What did you tell these women about us?"

CHAPTER THIRTY-SEVEN

IT TOOK US ABOUT HALF AN HOUR
to set up room number 3 for the Ural Soviet's
arrival.

"This is, like, *so* not going to work!" Varda said, set-
ting up the hotel's fancy silver forks and gold-edged
wineglasses. "Where do these little gold soup spoons
go—to the right of the plate, or above the bowl?"

"Shh! Quick—they're coming!"

For an instant we listened to the heavy *tramp-
tramp-tramp* of footsteps approaching. Grabbing
Varda, I dived under the narrow table, where the
heavy linen tablecloth barely hid us from view. There
was almost no room for us to move under there without being seen.

The door sprang open. I peeked out of the gap
between the edge of the tablecloth and the floor.
About a dozen pairs of polished boots strode into the
room.

"Take your seats, *tovaristchy*, we have the people's work to do!" the most forceful pair of shiny boots said.

The men sat down around the table in gilded arm-chairs. From underneath the table we heard forks clanging on plates, then crude chomping and slurping as they wolfed down food and drink.

The man in front of me suddenly crossed his legs. I snapped my head back—just in time to avoid getting my nose smashed by the tip of his boot.

BAM! Somebody had pounded a hard object—a gavel?—on the table, right over my head. My hand flew over my sore ear, but I did not cry out.

"This meeting of the Presidium of the Ural Soviet and the Ekaterinburg Cheka is called to order!" Mr. Shiny Boots said from the head of the table.

Suddenly the door burst open and another pair of boots stormed in.

"Comrade Avdeyev!" Mr. Shiny Boots said to the newcomer. "What are *you* doing here?"

The man plunked himself down at the table in an empty chair right in front of where Varda was hiding.

"I've heard about your plans for my charges! I cannot allow it! I have a sacred responsibility to protect—"

"The Ural Soviet has a special purpose in mind for the residents of Ipatiev House," Shiny Boots inter-rupted. "This purpose involves extreme measures that are at the forefront of our plans for them. You do not fit in with these plans. Comrade Avdeyev, you are dismissed from your position as commandant of Ipatiev! Effective immediately."

"But I—"

"No arguments, Avdeyev! You are too soft, you're a drunk—you have allowed too much familiarity with the prisoners."

Avdeyev stood up and angrily stomped his foot—right on Varda's knuckles! I quickly clapped my hand over her mouth, watching helplessly as her face turned red. She bit her lip and tears of pain ran down her cheeks.

"Dismiss me if you like," Avdeyev said, "but the whole world will condemn us as monsters if any harm comes to them!"

At this I listened even more closely. *Could he be talking about my family?*

"I do not need your permission to dismiss you, Comrade Avdeyev. Nor would I need your permission to send you and your wife and children to a labor camp in Siberia! Do you understand my meaning?"

We heard Avdeyev sigh, defeated.

"Yes, Comrade Beloborodov." Avdeyev turned away from the table, then shuffled slowly across the marble floor like a beaten dog. He slipped out the door.

"Comrade Yurovsky!" Shiny Boots Beloborodov announced. Another man, presumably Yurovsky, sprang to his feet. "You will take over as commandant of the House of Special Purpose—beginning today."

"Thank you, comrade! I intend to prove myself worthy of the Ural Soviet's trust." He sat down.

The man they called Yurovsky dropped his fountain pen, and it rolled under the table. His stubby hand patted the floor under the table in all directions—but the pen was just out of his grasp. I saw the tablecloth rustle.

Oh, no! He was going to duck his head under the table!

Thinking quickly, I nudged the pen toward his hand with the tip of my foot.

He got it! Thank God!

"Now. On to our primary order of business," Shiny Boots said.

Somebody in the room was wearing so much cologne it smelled like an explosion in a perfume factory. An uncontrollable tickle started inside my nose. Panicking, I nudged Varda, pointing toward my twitching nose. Now she looked panicked too.

KA-BOOM!

Artillery fire! Perhaps only a few dozen versts away!

Varda and I flinched at the sound—and she struck her head on the vibrating "ceiling" of the table. The glasses and silverware above us rattled like the ghost of Peter the Great walking on the bones of the dead. A trickle of red wine dripped steadily from the table, forming a thick red pool on the floor in front of me.

"As you can hear, the White Army and Czech

Legions are getting nearer Ekaterinburg by the hour," Beloborodov said to the others. "The Revolution is in mortal danger! We can no longer wait for central authority in Moscow to act."

Finally I couldn't hold it in any longer. I looked at Varda helplessly—and I sneezed.

"God bless you!" several of the men said to each other at once. I was terrified that they'd look under the table—or that I'd have a nosebleed. But, fortunately, neither thing happened.

"Safarov!" Beloborodov said. "Have you drawn up the resolution?"

"Yes, comrade!"

"Then read it to us."

We heard the rustling of paper. Then a man stood and recited to the group.

"'The Ural Regional Soviet categorically refuses to take the responsibility for transferring Nicholas Romanov in the direction of Moscow as has been suggested, and considers it necessary therefore to liquidate him.'"

Varda grasped my hand, her eyes seeking mine. She could not understand what the man had said, but there was no mistaking the look of horror on my face.

"'There is grave danger that Citizen Romanov will fall into the hands of the Czechoslovaks and other counterrevolutionaries and be used to their benefit. We cannot ignore this question. We face a critical moment in our revolutionary path: We must move forward. We cannot turn away from our duty to the revolution. Romanov's family and those who have elected to remain with him and share his imprisonment must all be liquidated at the same time. . . .'"

My sisters and mama, too—just as Varda had said! Holy Mother of God!

"'These liquidations will take place no later than July 16.'"

July 16? That's only three days from now!

"Good, comrade," Beloborodov said. "All in favor of the resolution, say 'aye.'"

"Aye!" repeated a chorus of strong voices.

"All opposed?"

Silence.

Then the *BAM!* of the gavel—like an arrow through my heart.

"The resolution is approved. I will sign on behalf of the presidium." We heard the sound of a paper sliding across the tabletop, then a pen scratching. "Goloshchokin, bring this resolution to Moscow for immediate approval by Lenin and Sverdlov."

"Yes, comrade!" came the reply. "I will go without delay."

BAM!

"Meeting adjourned!"

CHAPTER THIRTY-EIGHT

Ekaterinburg
Saturday, 13 July 1918

WE SPRINTED DOWN VOZNESENSKY PROSPEKT,
pausing only to catch our breath. I turned my ear
to a sound so foreign that I barely remembered or
recognized it.

Music!

A band in the gazebo played a romantic waltz.
Couples strolled the Ekaterinburg Municipal Gardens
arm in arm, gazing into each other's eyes. They
laughed, cooing to each other like doves. Some of
them even danced!

Life seemed so normal it might have been any
Saturday in a small Russian town before the revolution. Didn't these foolish *mouzhiks* know that their
country was in the middle of a bloody civil war, with
armies pounding at their gates? How could they ignore
the dull distant thudding of heavy guns, marking the
downbeat of their waltz like a big bass drum? Didn't
they know that their tsar and his family were about

to be murdered—*da*, murdered in cold blood right under their ignorant noses!—their *sudba* written in blood?

But maybe, I realized, they did not care. Or maybe they danced so joyfully precisely because they did not know what doom tomorrow might bring. It is just as my mother said: Happiness is fleeting and must be grabbed with both hands while it lasts.

"Did the Bolsheviks say where Ipatiev House is?" Varda asked me as we paused near the garden gate. I had already translated for her everything the Ural Soviet had discussed in room number 3.

"*Nyet.* But should not be difficult to find out," I said, grabbing her hand and pulling her along. "We must hurry!"

We stopped a few people on the street to ask them where Ipatiev House was, but none of them seemed to hear my question.

Then we passed a crooked-backed man who was carrying a heavy cloth sack on his shoulder. He was squinting at a pile of envelopes clutched in his hand. A toy-size dog was alternately yipping at him and boldly nipping at his heels, then backing away, terrified.

"A mailman!" Varda said. "Ask him—he'll know!"

"*Izvini*, can you tell me where I can find Ipatiev House?"

The mailman's eyes darted from side to side. Then he stared down at the pavement, as if he expected to see ants crawling out from between the cracks.

"I have never heard of this place. Never!"

"But it's right here in Ekaterinburg. Surely you must—"

The man walked away from us—backward, like a picture show unspooling in reverse. Then he dropped his pile of letters, turned, and ran.

"Wait! You forgot your—"

Varda picked up the letters and handed them to me. I was about to toss them away, but noticed that one of them was addressed to Commandant Avdeyev—the man who'd just been fired by the Ural Soviet. And it was sent to him care of Ipatiev House!

"Look! The address!" I said to Varda. Of course, she could not read it in Russian. "It's here on Voznesensky Prospekt!"

We bolted down the street.

Across the square from Ascension Cathedral was a corner house with no number on it. But the other houses were numbered, so I was sure that this must be the place.

One look at Ipatiev House and my heart dropped into my shoes. I knew that not even Joshua and his trumpet could make those thick stone walls come tumbling down. The two-story house was surrounded by a high sharp-pointed fence. I could barely see the tops of the second floor windows above it—and the glass had been whitewashed over, so we could not see in. Angry-looking guards carrying Mausers were posted at several locations outside the palisade. I had little doubt that other soldiers would be stationed within the gates as well.

Bong! Bong! Bong!

The cathedral bell tolled the hour. I glanced up at the church tower. A machine gun was set up there, aimed directly at Ipatiev House across the street. Had the House of Special Purpose been holding all the gold in the Russian empire instead of the Romanov prisoners, it could not have been better guarded.

We walked around the house a few times, trying to seem like lovers out for a casual stroll. But in fact I was studying every inch of "Fortress Ipatiev." *There must be some way in!* But there was not a hole in that fence big enough for a mouse.

"Alexei," Varda whispered, "that guard over there is giving us the evil eye. They're getting suspicious. We'd better move along for a while."

"*Nyet!* I must *think*!"

"You there!" the guard shouted at us. "What are you doing?"

"Inspecting for termites!" I said.

"Very funny. Move along!"

I just scowled at him.

"We'll go somewhere else to think," Varda whispered, pulling me away. "You can't do your family any good if we get caught!"

We crossed to the other side of the square, and I took a long look back at the House of Special Purpose.

I was still the tsarevich—da! This, no revolution,

no army could ever take away from me. But today I felt like just an ordinary boy. A boy in a world of men who were bigger, stronger, smarter than he. Just a sickly boy with the bleeding disease, skinny like a rooster on half rations. I was still two weeks short of my fourteenth birthday. And with my family held prisoner in a fortress that even God himself could not breach, it was suddenly I, not my papa the tsar, who held the whole miserable world up on his shoulders. My parents and sisters were in the hands of the devil. They had only seventy-two hours left on this earth—unless, by the grace of God, I could come up with some way to set them free.

CHAPTER THIRTY-NINE

Sunday, 14 July 1918

WE SLEPT THAT NIGHT

at an ammunition dump in Ekaterinburg—our heads resting against a white powdery heap of saltpeter that was softer than the pillows at Stavka. I had not wanted to waste any time sleeping. But Varda insisted we could plan better after a good night's rest. I was tripping over my own feet from exhaustion—so, at last, I had to admit she was right.

That night I dreamed that I was dancing Pet-rouchka—and leaped so high I floated off into the sky, where someone I knew greeted me in heaven—on angel's wings.

"Ah—welcome, Alyosha!" Father Grigory said, kissing me on both cheeks. "Surprised to find me here? I spend some time with devil, but he get sick of me, send me here!"

"Yiowwwww!"

Varda and I awoke to the rude shock of cold water pouring on our heads—followed by loud laughter.

"That'll teach you!" a soldier said, tossing away an empty bucket. "This is no place for children—go away!"

The water was filthy, and stung our eyes. We scrambled to our feet and ran away.

Within minutes we were back outside Ipatiev House.

As the cathedral bell tolled seven times, several nuns carrying baskets of goods approached the wooden fence. The guards smiled as if their faces weren't used to it, opened the fence gate for the nuns, and let them pass inside.

"There must be some way to get my family out of there," I muttered, inspecting every footprint in the dust and crack in the fence.

"Alexei," Varda whispered. "Will you stop with the Sherlock Holmes stuff already? The guards might catch us."

I stopped dead in my tracks and grabbed her by both arms.

"*Sherlock Holmes*? That's it!"

I pulled her away to a bench in the square across the street, where we could talk more freely.

"What's wrong?" Varda said.

"'A Scandal in Bohemia!'"

"Huh?"

"Is title of story my papa read to us! In story, Sherlock Holmes trick woman to show him where she hide secret photograph."

"Alexei, do you really think we should be wasting time yapping about books when your family is in danger?"

"Listen! Sherlock Holmes goes to woman's house in disguise—pretends he is injured. Woman has him carried inside house, Holmes asks window be opened for air. Then friend Watson throws smoke bomb through window, shouts, 'Fire!' Woman thinks her house is on fire, goes straight to place where precious photo is hidden. Now Sherlock Holmes knows where photo is!"

"Good for Sherlock Holmes. So?"

"You do not see? We get someone inside Ipatiev House, fake sudden illness or injury. They gasp for air, ask for window open. I throw smoke bomb through open window from outside, shout 'fire!' Bolsheviks *go straight for what is most precious to them*: hidden Romanov family. They want family dead, but not from fire. They bring everyone outside, tsar and family escape under cover of smoke!"

"Alexei, this is crazy! *Smoke bombs?*"

"It work for Sherlock Holmes! You are scientist, da? You know how to make?"

"Well, I do, actually. The kids set smoke bombs off all the time in the boys' bathroom at school. But—but that's not the point! I—"

"Good! We save my family!" I took Varda by the hands and danced her around. As I spun her around in the mazurka, she couldn't help but laugh.

"Alexei," Varda said, "how are we going to find somebody to get inside that house?"

I glanced toward the Ipatiev gate, where the nuns were now exiting, nodding farewell to the guards, baskets empty. I turned back to Varda and smiled.

"Welcome to Ekaterinburg, 'Sister Varda.'"

We knocked on the door to Novotikhvinsky Convent.

"Yes?" a cautious voice answered through the heavy oak door.

"We are two strangers seeking refuge with the holy sisters of the church."

After all, it was true. My parents had taught me never to lie—especially to nuns.

The door crept open a crack, and a kindly blue eye peered at me. Then the door opened all the way.

"Welcome, my children," the nun said. And then she did the most extraordinary thing. She fainted.

"I'm so sorry!" I said some minutes later to the mistress of the convent, who had come rushing into the room when she'd heard the other nun hit the floor. "I didn't mean to frighten her."

"No need to apologize, Your Highness," the mistress replied as she kneeled, waving the smelling salts under her holy sister's nose. "You are not to blame. But you can imagine the shock! We all thought the tsarevich was dead." She pointed to a portrait of me with my family that was hanging on the convent wall. "And your poor family is being held prisoner. . . ."

"Yes, we know. Have you spoken with them?"

The mistress helped the other nun—now awake, but still groggy—to the couch, patting her hand.

"Only briefly. The Bolsheviks permit us to bring baskets of food to them every morning at seven—a few eggs, some milk, perhaps a few grapes. Everything is rationed now. I only wish we had more to give them!"

"Do they—do they seem well?"

She sighed.

"As well as can be expected. Your parents look terribly tired and worried, of course. And your sister Olga, too. They know the danger they are in. The other girls . . . seem more carefree. Perhaps they are too young to really understand. Sister Antonina here even saw Grand Duchess Marie flirting with several of the guards."

How like our "Mashka"! My clever sister Marie— trying to win the guards' sympathy with her charm and beauty! But I knew it would not change my family's terrible *sudba*. I was their only hope.

"Do they . . . ever speak of me?"

Sister Antonina sat up on the couch and looked at me.

"Once I overheard the tsarina say to the tsar, 'If only our dear Sunbeam were here! The days would not seem so long!'"

"Da!" I said. "Mama calls me 'Sunbeam,' sometimes."

The convent mistress nodded toward Varda, then extended her hand to both of us.

"I am Sister Agnes, and over there are Sisters Antonina and Maria." We nodded at them. "Who is this nice young lady with you?"

"My cousin Varda, from America."

Varda, looking a little bewildered, smiled at the nuns with a little wave, and they smiled gently back.

"We need your help," I said to the holy sisters.

"We pray for your family—every day," Sister Agnes said. "It is a crime what the Bolsheviks have done to them. A crime against God!"

She crossed herself, then patted the couch next to Sister Antonina so that we would sit next to her.

"Now, my children," Sister Agnes said, with a surprisingly conspiratorial glint in her eye. "Tell us exactly what you would like us to do."

CHAPTER FORTY

Monday, 15 July 1918. Morning.

THE BELL OF ASCENSION CATHEDRAL tolled once, twice—seven times. Two nuns strode up to the fence gate of Ipatiev House and knocked sharply. A slovenly-looking guard opened the gate and looked them over.

Please, Holy Mother, let nothing go wrong!

Through the field glasses I'd kept courtesy of the Red Army, I studied the scene from a safe distance. Would the guard let them through?

Sister Maria gestured to the other nun. I knew what she'd be saying to the guard: "Sister Antonina is ill today, so sent Sister Catherine in her place."

The guard studied the nun called Sister Catherine suspiciously for a moment. I held my breath. Then—thank God!—he let them pass. In less than thirty seconds Varda, doing a very good imitation of a Russian Orthodox nun who'd taken a vow of silence, would be inside the house. Within another minute she would pretend to faint from the stifling heat of summer. What man would doubt the actions of a pretty nun?

Once Varda was carried upstairs to Ipatiev's only couch, Sister Maria would beg for the side window to be opened to give the fainting victim some fresh air. The instant I saw the window open, that would be my cue.

The day before, Varda had prepared two smoke bombs in tin cans. All I had to do was light the matchsticks we'd sunk into the material inside the cans. I'd throw one smoke bomb over the Ipatiev House fence and through the open upstairs window, the other into the street, and when their fuses burned down—*KA-BOOM!*

You may be wondering how we made smoke bombs. Varda used the convent oven to melt together six parts saltpeter, which we'd stolen from the ammunition dump, with four parts . . .

Well, do not expect me to give you the details! The formula includes a very common, harmless ingredient found in every kitchen. But Varda warned me that the final mixture could be very dangerous in the hands of foolish people or small children. You can imagine how Sister Antonina wrung her hands as she watched us use the convent oven for our plans!

Varda said the bombs would make enough smoke to cover a whole city block. This would give us plenty of time to lead my family down the street and escape into the woods, where Sisters Agnes and Antonina—God bless them!—were in the convent's truck, waiting to drive all of us away.

I watched the house, waiting nervously for my chance. I knew that inside, at this very moment, Varda would be presenting a basket of eggs to my family. She'd draw their attention to one of them, and Sister Maria would say that they should eat it immediately, it had come from a special chicken! *Special?* No joke! This egg's yolk and white had been blown out through a tiny hole—like for making painted Easter eggs. Inside, rolled up into a tiny scroll, was a note for my parents on which I'd written: "Tsarevich alive and well. When you hear 'fire!' run for northwest corner of square, where friends will take you to safety." I'd signed the note "Sunbeam," so my family would know it was from me. Crack the egg open—and they'd find it!

I watched the attic window.

At last! The window opened!

I struck a match and lit the fuses on the smoke bombs, then rushed toward the house.

Suddenly a dog came running around to the side of the house, nosing around for a good place to pee. It spotted me and froze, like pointing game. Then, ears flattening against its head, the dog crouched playfully, wagging its tail in happy recognition. This wasn't "a dog"—it was *my* dog.

Joy!

I held up my hand, silently pleading with him.

Oh my God, Joy—please, no! Don't!

RRRRUFF! RRRRUFF!

He bounded toward me, knocking me over and licking my face like I was ice cream.

I was thrilled to see him again, of course, but his timing might have been better. Four Ipatiev guards, alerted by the barking, barreled toward me from their posts. They pulled a yelping Joy off me and yanked me to my feet.

Naturally, being found with two lit bombs in my hands did not argue well for my innocence. The guards blew out the fuses and placed me under arrest.

CHAPTER FORTY-ONE

I STOOD SILENTLY IN THE FRONT ROOM of Ipatiev House, a rifle butt pressed roughly into my shoulder blade. Varda and Sister Maria were being led downstairs by two other guards. My Little Peasant was shaking with fear. With all my being, how I wanted to help her! But I turned away, eyes staring straight ahead.

It may seem cruel that I pretended not to know her—and, da, it nearly broke my heart. But you must understand. I knew that if the Bolsheviks guessed that Varda had been part of my plan, she too would have been taken prisoner—or worse.

"We caught the boy red-handed, Captain Lepa," one of my captors said to a nasty-looking guard, thrusting me toward him. "The little bastard was going to throw *these* through the window." He handed his captain the smoke bombs.

"Good work, comrade!" Lepa jerked his head toward Varda. "Verhas, who is that girl? I don't remember seeing her here before."

"Just one of the sisters who come daily from the convent. Replacing one who is ill."

He turned his attention back to me.

"We must find out if the bomber was acting alone or is part of a counterrevolutionary conspiracy." Lepa planted me right in front of Varda. "Sister, the people demand answers: Is this boy from the town? Do you know him?"

It was clear she understood the general idea of the captain's question.

I stared at Varda now, pleading silently with her to do what was best for her. Oh, she argued with me, she protested—I could feel this strongly in my mind. But at last, thank the Lord, I silently persuaded her, and she reluctantly surrendered to my wishes.

"*Nyet*," Varda said to the Captain.

"Get the nuns out of here," he said to the guards.

As Sister Maria and Varda were rushed out the door, my American cousin craned her neck around for one last look at me. The pitiful look in her eyes pulled at my heart like a troika drawn by the mightiest horses. But we both knew that there was nothing I could do now that would not endanger her life.

She was gone.

Suddenly, a young guard watching from the doorway caught my eye, gasped, and dropped to his knees. With a trembling hand, he swept off his cap and bowed his head with deep reverence.

"Your Highness!"

"Kabanov!" another guard said. "For Christ's sake, get up!"

The young man rose slowly to his feet. He looked at me sadly, and I could see he had tears in his eyes. I recognized him as one of Papa's grenadiers before the war. I nodded toward him, giving a small smile of gratitude.

"Mother of God, it's the heir!" another guard said. "Get Yurovsky!"

CHAPTER FORTY-TWO

FOR A MOMENT, I BARELY RECOGNIZED HER. Her hair had turned white as the Snow Maiden's. That still-beautiful face was etched now: a map showing the path to years of pain and worry. Though she sat in a wheelchair, she struggled unsteadily to her feet, reaching toward me like a man in the desert who'd caught sight of his last glass of water. But was I a mirage, or was I real?

"Mama!"

I fell, sobbing, into her open arms.

"Who are you, young man? Tell me who you are before my poor heart dies of hope."

I had forgotten—I was two years older now, and looked it; my voice had changed.

"It's me, Mama. Your Alexei."

She looked uncertain, confused. She sniffed my hair, inhaling deeply, and then the most peaceful smile lit up the darkened shadows of her face. Like the midnight sun.

At last my family was together again. My captors had taken me to the five rooms on the main floor, where my parents and sisters, Dr. Botkin, and several loyal servants who had gone into exile with them—our cook Kharitonov and Leonka the kitchen boy, Mama's lady-in-waiting Anna Demidova, and our footman Mr. Trupp—were being held. And even though I knew, as my family did not, what terrible *sudba* was in store for us, for this moment I could not have been more happy. This is what the Bolsheviks in their cold-eyed hatred would never understand. They who did not love God, did not trust in him as we did—did not know love even in their own families, else why would they leave their own at home just to torment mine? There was nothing they could take away from us, as long as we were together. Nothing!

Papa, dressed in a common colonel's uniform, embraced me silently, his heart too full to speak his feelings. And if ever I had even a moment's doubt about who was the father of my blood, I knew for certain who was the father of my heart.

My sisters fluttered around me, chirping answers—and questions—through their tears.

"We thought the Bolsheviks had stolen you!"

"My arm circles all the way around your waist—just skin and bones!"

"Felix said you'd just vanished—he'd thought you'd fallen through the ice and drowned!"

"Look at you! Our handsome young man will slay all the girls!"

"I'm sorry, I'm a little fool. Forgive me for every time I called you 'pest'!"

My sisters had always been careful not to hug me too tightly, for fear of bruising me. But today, in our happiness and relief at seeing one another, none of us worried about this.

I heard a noise at the door, and turned around.

"Zhillie!"

We stood a moment, just staring at each other. Then I bounded toward him like Joy, and embraced him. Gilliard was always shy and formal. As I released him, he took a step back, wiping his eye on the cuff of his sleeve. He cleared his throat a couple of times before he could get any words out.

"Alexei, have you been keeping up with your studies?"

"No, Zhillie. You know I am a lazy schoolboy."

Tugging at his pointy beard, he cracked a smile. Then his expression became very serious.

"They are sending me away tomorrow. I demanded to remain here with your family, but I am a Swiss national. They insisted I must leave."

I nodded. Actually, I was more relieved than disappointed that the Bolsheviks were taking him away. Gilliard would have a chance to escape, and would not share our *sudba*.

As for Varda, I knew that Sister Maria would take

her back to the convent and make sure she was safe. But this did not stop me from thinking about her, worrying about her, needing her. In every way, she was my family too.

That night, Mashka and Tatiana sat at the parlor piano, playing and singing. But they looked frightened and ill rather than joyful. Two guards, reeking of vodka, sat pressed close on either side of them. One of the men was turning music pages with long dirty fingers. They forced my sisters to sing revolutionary songs.

"Louder!" Dirty Fingers said, nudging a sickened Mashka in the ribs. "Play 'Let's Forget the Old Regime' and 'You Fell Victim to the Struggle'!"

"Leave her alone!" I said, lunging at him. The man tossed me off like a flea.

"You think you Romanovs can still tell us what to do? Now we ration your food and spit in your soup!"

The men laughed.

One of them told a low and disgusting joke, the sort one hears in an army barracks. Turning pale, Tatiana ran from the room. Mashka stared at the man scornfully.

"Why are you not disgusted with yourselves when you use such shameful words? Do you imagine that you can woo a well-born woman with such witticisms and have her be well disposed toward you? Be refined and respectable men and then we can get along."

As I watched the men slink off in shame like scolded hounds, I was full of pride in my sister.

I crossed to the end of the main floor, and heard my mother quietly reminding Olga and Anastasia that it was time to take care of their "candy and medicines." I thought this strange, until I saw what they were *really* up to. They were sewing our family's diamonds and emeralds into the hems of the girls' skirts and corsets, and inside our shirts, pillows, and hat rims. If my sisters ever got separated from the rest of the family, Mama knew that they would be able to sell off their hidden jewels—perhaps bribe their way out of trouble—and be all right. But neither my mother nor my sisters had any idea what was really in store for them. And that no bribe would be enough to save them now.

"Mama, hasn't *anyone* tried to come to our rescue?" I whispered to her. She shook her head sadly. "The Americans? Our cousin King George of England, perhaps?"

My mother shook her head again. "There was . . . some talk. Nothing happened. Nobody wants to take the risk of giving the hated Romanovs refuge."

"What about the Germans?"

"I'd rather die at the hands of the Bolsheviks than be rescued by the Germans!"

Later I knocked on the door of Gilliard's room. He opened it, and I shut the door behind me.

"Zhillie?"

"Yes?"

"Will you do something for me?"

"You know I will. If I can."

I sat on the bed and lowered my voice in case the Bolsheviks were listening at the door.

"If—if anything ever happens to us—to *me*—please come back to this house. Once the White Army has taken over Ekaterinburg, it will be safe to return here. I am going to leave a book for you inside the piano bench. I want you to take good care of it."

Gillliard didn't try to argue with me by saying we'd all be fine. He had never lied to me. He wouldn't start now.

Gilliard looked me straight in the eye. "You have my word."

CHAPTER FORTY-THREE

Tuesday, 16 July 1918

I'D SPENT THE REST OF MONDAY glued to my family, my questions tumbling out in torrents: "Where did they take you?" "Did anyone harm you?" "What happened to Grandma Minnie, Cousin Felix, and my sailor-nanny Nagorny?" "Where is Uncle Misha?" No matter who I asked about, their answers sounded all the same, like the droning litany of the mass: "We don't know," "Dead, I fear," or "Taken away." Catching up on the lives of my parents and sisters, I tried to live a year and a half in a single day. My face was a mask, behind which I hid from them the terrible truth: The next day would be our last.

It may seem strange to you that my family did not ask me where I had been. Perhaps they would have, in time. But all that mattered to them now was that I had returned to them safely, and we were all together again. They had even kept my clothes for me here, hoping that I would come back to them one day. But I sensed that they had learned the hard way—as I was quickly learning myself—that hearing answers to questions sometimes brought more pain than one could bear.

I'd stayed up all night on the fifteenth, my pen on fire, racing against the clock to finish writing this book. You see, it now had a different purpose from when I had begun. This was no longer just the story of my life, the boy who would one day be tsar of all the Russias. It was our legacy—our insurance against the hateful lies that would be told about the Romanovs after we were gone. They would say my father was cruel, a bloody dictator. They would say my mother was cold and heartless, and my sisters spoiled and useless. That we never knew pain nor sacrifice. They would say that Rasputin was just an evil man who controlled every decision of the tsar, and was kept at the palace as the tsarina's pet—for no reason but her amusement. They would say we danced while the peasants ate dirt.

Today, the morning of the sixteenth, dawned hot and humid, heavy with portent.

Gilliard, clutching a small satchel, stood before me. He opened his mouth to speak, but then looked at his feet and said nothing.

"Goodbye, Zhillie," I said. "Live strong."

He raised an eyebrow at me, looking puzzled, then pleased.

"Russia does not know what it has lost," he said. "Alexei Nikolaevich Romanov, you would have made a great tsar."

I stood tall, more grateful to him than words could say.

We shook hands, and then he went down the stairs and was gone.

In other ways today did not seem different from the day before. My family followed what they told me was now their regular routine. The day started with our praying together, just as we had at home. We ate what the Bolsheviks allowed us—some black bread, a glass of tea. Then at ten, Yurovsky, the commandant, lined us up like army troops for inspection. It was really just a head count to make sure no one had escaped. There was a changing of the guard every six hours. Sister Maria and Sister Antonina had arrived promptly at seven, carrying baskets of eggs and milk to supplement our meager rations. As she was handing me a basket, Sister Antonina managed to whisper in my ear, "Varda is safe." This lifted a great weight from my spirits.

My family did not suspect that this was to be their last day. True, they seemed worried and depressed— but I imagine they had been so for quite some time. I kept staring at the guards' faces, searching into their souls. *What kind of man are you? Or are you nothing but a beast? Are you the one who will shoot us? Are you cold-blooded and cowardly enough to pull the trigger on my beautiful mother and sisters?*

The hours ticked by, and the bell in Ascension Cathedral tolled our *sudba*. But when evening came and still nothing had happened to us, I dared hope that perhaps the Ural Soviet had had a change of heart. *Maybe they are not so beastly, after all,* I thought. *Maybe they cannot bring themselves to shoot this kindly and devoted family man whom God has made their tsar. Maybe they cannot steel themselves to slaughter defenseless women and children.*

At ten fifteen that night, Dr. Botkin was sitting at a desk, writing a letter—to his family, I supposed. I saw him take off his glasses and wipe his eyes, then continue writing with a heavy sigh. Perhaps somehow he knew this letter would be his last.

I rubbed my knee—it was swollen and hurting from when Joy had knocked me down.

Then I heard music coming from my breast pocket. The telephone! In all the excitement of seeing my family again, I had forgotten all about it.

I ducked into a closet, pulled the door shut behind me, and pressed the telephone button.

"Varda!"

"Please, Alexei. Come back with me to the future! Don't you see? There is nothing more you can do for your family now."

I looked into the telephone screen at her lovely face. Those eyes, blue like the Neva, that were a sparkling mirror of my own. But now her eyes had a touch of red, and I could tell that she had been weeping.

"You know how much I care for you," I said. "But cannot leave family."

"Then we'll take them with us!"

"*Nyet*. Mama and Papa would never leave Mother Russia, Romanovs do not run away. They need me here. Cannot let them die alone."

"They won't be alone! They have each other! What about me?"

Her words pulled at my heart. In all my life the hardest thing I ever had to do was close it—just a little—against her.

"Varda, please. I beg you! Try to understand. If leave family now, world will say last tsarevich was coward."

"I don't care what the world says! I need you, Alexei!"

"I know. Need you too."

We were silent for a moment. Then I said: "What would you do? Put self in my place."

She shut her eyes for a moment, then opened them.

"When my father was dying, those last days, I slept on a cot just outside his room. I got so I knew how many times he breathed in a minute. When he skipped even one, it was like *I* had stopped breathing. That morning, I held his hand for hours, thinking maybe if I just held on tight enough and didn't let go, he'd never slip away. . . ."

"So you know where I must be."

She sighed. "Yes."

My telephone started flashing a message.

"What means this, 'Battery low'?"

"It means—it means we're out of time, Alexei."

"I see," I said. "Good-bye, Little Peasant."

I leaned toward my telephone screen, as she did toward hers. We kissed the glass between our lips.

Then the screen went black.

CHAPTER FORTY-FOUR

1:30 A.M. Wednesday, 17 July 1918

WE WERE ALL ASLEEP.

A knock on the bedroom door at the House of Special Purpose yanked me rudely back from my beautiful dreams of Varda. Mama, face creased from her pillow, hair down around her shoulders like a young girl's, went to answer it.

"Yurovsky says there's trouble in the town, they must move us to a place of greater safety," Dr. Botkin told her. "It would be dangerous to be in the upper rooms if there is shooting in the streets. He says we must dress quickly and go downstairs."

My mother frowned.

"That awful man could not have told us this at a decent hour? All right, Doctor. Tell him I'll wake the children and we'll be down as soon as we're dressed."

The threat to Ekaterinburg from advancing White and Czech forces had been as great yesterday as today. If Yurovsky was waking us in the middle of the night,

I knew it was not for our safety, but for some "special purpose."

My hands shook so while I dressed that I had trouble buttoning my military shirt.

"Here, Little Man," Olga said, coming to my aid. "I'll do that for you."

Olga probably thought I was just nervous about the armies marching toward Ekaterinburg. And this is just what I'd hoped she would think. Since there was no escape for any of us, it would be best if they did not know what was about to happen to them. *Please, Holy Mother, give me the strength not to betray my feelings!*

As Olga did the buttons on my shirt, she smiled at me—that gentle, motherly smile of the big sister that I had known since she'd wiped the infant's spittle from my bib. I bit my lip, trying not to weep. How it tore at my heart to think she would never have children of her own!

I was first to go downstairs, and Yurovsky and the guards had not yet entered from their posts. I sat, alone with my thoughts, writing in this book, waiting to meet my *sudba*. I pressed the button on my telephone. "Battery low," but it was still working. Perhaps long enough to—

"ILUVU4EVA," I typed, and pressed send.

There was no answer.

My family was now gathered all around me. My eyes passed from one dear, dear face to another, engraving them into my memory. Papa with his quiet strength and unguarded eyes that dared to let you see into the very depths of his gentle soul. Mama whose Snow Maiden courage showed in the coolly determined set of her jaw, but whose meltingly warm smile was a special gift kept only for her husband and us children. Olga, facing life square on, brave enough to lead armies like Joan of Arc. Tatiana, "the governor," who had inherited my mother's sense of duty, and wisely steered us away from childish nonsense unsuited to the offspring of a tsar. Dear Anastasia, our sprite of mischief, who took the hot air out of anyone too puffed up with their own importance. And lovely Marie, our "Mashka," a warm and feminine flirt, who still stood firmly on the rock of principle when her noble sense of decency was offended.

Dr. Botkin stood calmly wiping his eyeglasses on a handkerchief. This wonderful man who had left his own family, to take such good care of me and mine. And there stood our loyal servants who had bravely followed my family here, willing to make our *sudba* theirs: Papa's valet Trupp, Mama's maid Anna—clutching two small pillows like a child's teddy bears—and our cook Kharitonov. We'd been told that Leonka the kitchen boy had been taken home by his uncle. God help him, I hoped it was true.

"Cross the courtyard and go downstairs into the room in the basement," the black-bearded man they called Yurovsky ordered us, his hand nervously tapping the right pocket of his uniform. I noticed the crescent moon shape of a small object, its outline showing through the pocket fabric. "You will be safer there."

Everyone turned to go.

I crossed the room, and pretended to be looking through the piano music inside the bench.

"Come, Alexei," Papa said, noticing I was limping. He held out his strong arms to lift and carry me one last time, as he had thousands of times before. As he had carried the whole of Mother Russia—the whole suffering world—on his shoulders.

"In a minute, Papa."

"Hurry up, boy!" Yurovsky snapped at me over his shoulder.

My telephone made music from my pocket. A message flashed on its screen.

"ILUVU4EVA2."

My heart leaped like Nijinsky. *Varda!*

"Battery dead."

The words winked out. And with them, all my hopes and dreams.

Putting the telephone back in my breast pocket, I scribbled these final words. In the next second I will slip this testament under the sheet music for Mozart's Requiem, then limp toward my father's outstretched arms.

They are calling me again. *Do svidaniya*, I must go!

At the threshold of our grave, I pray for my family and our enemies. May God grant

peace

to

✝   ✝   ✝

VARDA'S EPILOGUE

by Varda Ethel Rosenberg

1.

New York
December 2010

"I am Anatole Gilliard. Are you Mademoiselle Varda Ethel Rosenberg?"

The guy in the suit and tie who stood shivering at the door of our apartment stared at me with pop-eyed eagerness, like someone selling Scientology, or one of those people who wants money to save the rain forest. He tugged on his little polka-dotted bow tie, which was pressing against the Adam's apple on his skinny neck.

My mother told me that opening the door for a stranger in New York was dumber than burnt toast. But for the past week—ever since I'd left Alexei and his family to die back in 1918—I'd been hanging out back at home, doing nothing but crying my guts out and watching reruns of *Bewitched*. If this guy at the door was some new kind of wimpy-looking axe murderer, I was too miserable to care.

"Yeah, I'm Varda," I said. "Look, write us a letter if you want money, we don't do door-to-door spam."

I started to slam the door in his face. But before I could, he pushed a little book into my hands—this book. It was worn at its leather edges, and the fancy gold lettering was chipping off. But I could still make out the title: *The Curse of the Romanovs* by Alexei Romanov.

"I am the great-great-great-grandson of Pierre Gilliard," the man said with a French accent and a little bow. "Before the tragedy, Alexei ask Pierre to make certain this book reaches you."

"*My* Alexei?"

Anatole handed me one of those ritzy gold pens like you see in stores on Fifth Avenue, and a piece of paper with all kinds of legal stuff written on it.

"Sign here, *s'il vous plaît.*"

I signed, hoping it was just a receipt for the book and not a promise to become a Scientologist. I handed the paper and pen back to him. I had a million questions for this guy. But before I could even thank him, he was gone.

My mother wouldn't be home from work for several more hours. So I lay on my bed, gulping down everything that was in that book. And the more I read, the more sure I was. Nobody in the world could have written that book but my Alexei.

Alexei had known the Bolsheviks would never have allowed his story to be published while they ruled Russia. So he had left his book to the future—

to *me*—knowing that I'd do everything in my power to make sure it was published now that Russia was free. The world must finally learn the truth about him and his family. He had trusted me with his story. I would not let him down.

I'd come back to 2010 from 1918 only a few hours after I'd left. At least it was only a few hours from my mother's point of view. So she'd never even known I'd been gone.

That was only a week ago. She'd wanted to know where Alexei had gone, of course. But I knew she'd never have believed me if I'd told her the truth. So I said that his parents had called while she was at work, asking him to come home right away. We'd taken the bus out to the airport.

"He's gone back to Russia to be with his family," I said. "They really missed him."

Well, it wasn't exactly a lie.

When I couldn't eat or sleep, wouldn't go to school, and couldn't stop crying, my mother sort of understood. After all, she missed Alexei too.

Then came the big hemophilia science conference at the Roosevelt Hotel in New York. I'd been planning to go for months. I was hoping I might meet somebody there who'd give me research money to work on my gene therapy treatment, and let me work in their lab. But I was too depressed to go anywhere. Then my science teacher, Mrs. Gentian, actually called me up on the phone. She gave me a whole *shpiel* about how important this conference was, how important she thought my research was. And somehow, I don't know how she did it, she talked me into going.

I arrived at the conference about an hour late. I'd missed the keynote speech—about the challenges of finding a gene therapy cure for hemophilia.

There was an old man in a wheelchair up on the stage. Some scientists from Johns Hopkins introduced him as Vasily Filatov, the oldest living hemophiliac. It was like he was some freak of nature, the Elephant Man or something. He was one hundred and six years old—and they said they were studying his body chemistry to figure out how he'd survived with the disease for so long. Even with all the great new treatments available, most hemophiliacs probably wouldn't be able to live past their sixties. The scientists figured maybe they could learn something from studying this guy that could help other hemophiliacs, or even lead to a cure.

The man in the wheelchair didn't say anything. He just smiled and waved at the crowd.

As they were wheeling him off the stage, he passed right by me—and suddenly grabbed me by the wrist.

"Varda," he said in a dry, raspy whisper.

How did he know my name?

I nodded.

"Must talk with you in private," he said.

I rolled the old man's rusty wheelchair into an empty conference room down the hall. He asked me to shut the door behind us. When I turned back to face him, his head leaned on his chest, as if he'd nodded off. I was going to slip out. But then his eyes popped open, and he stretched his wrinkly neck like a supersize tortoise coming out of his shell. As he leaned toward me, I caught a whiff of mothballs from his wool jacket.

"Alexei survived."

"*What?*"

"He escape murder."

If I'd been hooked up to an EKG, it would have been doing the mambo, but I tried not to show it.

"The murder? How—how do you know?"

"I knew tsarevich. I was there."

I did the math. If this guy was over one hundred years old . . . Yeah, I guess he could be telling the truth. And he was Russian.

I sat down across from him, ready to listen.

Vasily Filatov leaned back in his wheelchair, as if just trying to remember things took all of his energy. His eyes glazed over. It was like he'd gone into some kind of trance.

"Twenty-three stairs. Twenty-three stairs they go down to basement room at House of Special Purpose. Tsar carry Alexei in his arms. Tsarina walk with cane, her back hurts. In room, tsarina says to Yurovsky, 'Why is there no chair here? What, may we not sit?' So two chairs brought in: one for tsarina, other for Alexei. Family, servants, line up against wall, like posing for photograph. Yurovsky says, 'You must wait here for arrival of truck.' They think they will be taken to safe place. They do not suspect truth—but Alexei, *he* knows."

I nodded at him to continue, bracing myself—wanting to hear, dreading to hear.

"Yurovsky goes to check on truck. He returns—with nine, maybe ten men. Then Yurovsky order prisoners to stand. He take crinkled piece of paper from pocket, reads to them: 'In view of fact that your relatives continue their offensive against Soviet Russia, Presidium of Ural Soviet decide to sentence you to death.' Tsar says, 'Lord, oh, my God! Oh, my God, what is this?' Tsar turns to face family. 'Oh, my God! No!' All confused. Doctor Botkin says: 'So we are not to be taken anywhere?' Tsar turns back to Yurovsky. 'I can't understand you. Read it again, please.' Yurovsky reads order again. Tsarina and Olga cross themselves. 'What?' Tsar says. 'What?'

"'*This!*' Yurovsky says, pulling pistol from pocket. Then . . . bullets fly everywhere, deafening, smoke, screams—oh, the screams! My papa fall forward, I grab for him—"

As his voice broke off, tears rolled down the dry creases in the old man's face like rain in the desert. He pounded his clenched fist on the arm of his wheelchair.

"My God, I was useless—useless!"

The old man bent his head, covering his face with

both hands, while his bony torso shook with his sobs. I put my hand on his shoulder.

At last he looked up at me, blue eyes washed with tears and suddenly as clear as a young boy's.

"I am Alexei Romanov."

2.

"No!" I pulled away, stumbling, as the old man reached for my hand. "What? You think this is some kind of joke? You think this is funny?"

"Varda—my dear! Please—don't go!"

He held out his open hands to me. Wheeling on him furiously, I crouched down low so I could look him right in his lying eyes.

"People died—do you understand? *Real* people, with real feelings—and real relatives who loved them. You can't go around pretending—pretending like this is some kind of stupid game!"

"So I am liar. All right, believe this if you want to believe. But sit, listen to story. Make good story, old man's story. Please. Listen . . . is all I ask."

Well, he was one hundred and six. And a hemophiliac. I figured it wouldn't cost me much to humor him. I looked at my watch.

"Lunch'll be over soon. I'll give you ten minutes," I said, pulling up a chair.

He smiled, with the few teeth he had left.

"Will only take five."

He pressed his hands together, like for making a prayer.

"They found bones of tsar, his family, servants killed with them in Ekaterinburg. Da?"

"Yes, in the forest about thirty years ago."

"Were bones of Alexei ever found?"

I said nothing.

"Were they?"

"That—that doesn't prove anything!"

"Night of murder, firing squad shoots, bullets bounce off Romanovs' bodies. Murderers in shock, terrified—*What means this? Does God protect royal children? Is family immortal?* When shooting stops, I hear terrible moans. My parents, they were already in heaven. But my sisters and I—we were still alive!"

"After a firing squad? How?"

"So much smoke, noise, screams, confusion—like scene from hell, oh, you cannot imagine! Ten men, maybe more, shoot at eleven people in small room— this not firing squad, this chaos. They cannot see who they are shooting. But most of reason we survive was candy and medicines."

"What?"

"That's what Mama called our jewels. Before murders, girls sewed family diamonds into their corsets, underclothing, the pillows Anna hold. And more diamonds inside my jacket. Bullets don't go through diamonds. Killers see my sisters still alive, know must finish them off. So they fix bayonets to rifles, and—"

He wiped his eyes with his sleeve. "Forgive, please. That part, so horrible, I cannot speak."

"I understand."

"Men check bodies, make sure all are dead. Then through gunsmoke, I see one man, he's moving toward me. He watches my chest rise, fall—sees I still breathe. He aims gun close, only a foot from my chest. Fires one shot. *BOOM!* I feel hard hit in chest. I think I am dead, join family in heaven, da? But something in breast pocket blocks bullet. I find—I still breathe. I don't dare move, shut my eyes, pretend to be dead."

His voice grew weak. I leaned closer, straining to hear.

"They wrapped us in sheets, carry bodies to truck waiting outside. Drive truck through Koptyaki forest. The White Nights are over, is now dark as black bread. Road is rough, and muddy from rain. With every bump, my heart, my body, cries out in pain—but I make sure no cry come from my lips. The truck's engine make noise, it stalls, we are stuck in mud. They unload the bodies from the back. And when they go look for another truck—this, this is when I escape. I hide under bridge near railroad tracks, then follow tracks to Shartash station, next town. Only a few miles. There I spot Papa's former grenadier, Kabanov, guard from House of Special Purpose. He had run away too, unwilling to shoot us. And he helped me, bring me to his mama's house. They take care of me."

I stared at him, thinking. Could it be true? At last I sighed, shaking my head.

"You do not believe me, da? I do not blame! Who would believe story? When I tell people I am Tsarevich Alexei Romanov, the Soviets think boy is crazy, put me in—how do you say? My English now is very poor."

"Asylum. Mental institution."

"Da! Was there for many year. They forget all about me. Even when Bolsheviks no longer in power. I write many letters, no one listen. So I begin to lie. I say I am only Vasily Filatov, not tsarevich. Doctors decide I am sane. But I *still* can't get out—commitment papers, they are long lost. Maybe could have bribed my way out—with diamonds sewn inside jacket. But they were all I had left of my family! Finally, write directly to Russian president, wheels of bureaucracy turn. Last week, they let me go. Russian president saw my medical records, tells American scientists I am hemophiliac, one hundred and six years old. '*Wonder man,' how does he survive so long with terrible disease? Is medical miracle!* Of course I control my bleeding with mind, as Father Grigory did; is very rare ability, but is no miracle. Only God can make miracle. American scientists invite me here. I knew I find Varda here too."

I looked at my watch and stood up.

"Your five minutes are almost up. Look, I'm not saying I believe any of this. But if you're Alexei, you could have traveled into the future. Anytime you wanted! How come you didn't just escape after your family was dead? Why didn't you come to me?"

"I wanted to! I try—God, again and again! But after beautiful family murdered in front of my eyes, I was alive, da—but something within me was dead. It change me forever. The magic not work anymore."

I really didn't know what to say. But I could see that to him, his story was real.

"I'm sorry about your—I mean, it was terrible what happened to Alexei and his family. I can see you're really sad about it. No matter who you are." I looked at my watch. "Look, nice meeting you. There's another lecture about to start. I gotta go. I'll take you back to the auditorium, okay?"

I walked behind his chair and started wheeling him toward the door.

"Mr. Filatov? Don't be mad at me. Let's shake hands. Look, it was a great story, okay?"

His head was resting on his chest, he seemed to be sleeping again.

But he wasn't breathing.

I shook him.

"My God—Mr. Filatov!"

His lifeless hand opened, and an object tumbled from it: A Kevlar cell phone, dented by the bullet lodged in it, with the initials *VER* and a double helix.

I fell to my knees.

"Oh, my darling Alexei!"

Alexei Nikolaevich Romanov, the last tsarevich of Russia, was born in 1904. After four girls were born to the royal couple, the country finally had an heir, and his arrival was greeted with great joy. But within the royal household that joy soon turned to sorrow. Within six weeks of his birth, Alexei began bleeding at the place where his umbilical cord had been cut, severing him from his mother. It was immediately clear to royal court physician Dr. Botkin that the boy had inherited the tragic disease of hemophilia—which came from Tsarina Alexandra's side of the family.

Tsarevich Alexei, his parents, Tsar Nicholas II and Tsarina Alexandra ("Alix"), and his sisters, Grand Duchesses Olga, Tatiana, Marie ("Mashka"), and Anastasia, were the central figures in the last imperial family of the three-hundred-year dynasty of Romanov tsars who had ruled Russia. Some descendants of the Romanovs are still alive today, but they do not rule Russia, which now elects its leaders.

Nicholas Romanov, Alexei's father, was a well-intentioned man who adored his family. He and his wife Alix had one of the greatest loves of any royal couple known to history. They suited each other perfectly—where he was weak, she was strong—and where she was weak, he was strong.

But Nicky (as his wife called him) was rather shy, did not like confrontations, and viewed the Russian people like children for whom the tsar was "father." Nicky often said he was "just a plain, simple man," and wished he could be a simple farmer instead of an emperor. He was easily influenced, and it was once said of him: "Tsar Nicholas is like a feather pillow, he bore the impression of the last person to sit on him." So he was temperamentally unsuited to be a modern twentieth-century leader. He never seemed to fully understand just how angry many peasants and workers eventually became at their Russian leaders, and at him in particular. The people's main complaints included lack of ownership of land for peasants, food shortages, and unsafe working conditions, low pay, and long hours for workers in factories. Others, especially the educated classes, wanted political and civil rights. Russian Jews were forced to live in ghettos called shtetls, were restricted to certain professions, and were victims of pogroms—mass murders instigated by, or given tacit approval by, the government. There is much evidence that Nicholas II approved of the persecution of Jews, though he did not personally order Jewish massacres.

My own grandmother, a Jewess, fled Russia-Poland as a child around 1911, and came to the United States. Nicholas's grandfather, Alexander II, had been a reformer—so when Alexander was assassinated by a terrorist, the Romanov family concluded that it was better to crack down and be autocratic rulers than to allow the people more freedoms. Alexander's successor, Nicholas's father (Alexander III), ruled Russia with a strong hand. But when Nicholas himself became tsar in 1894, Russia was modernizing and changing—and to many Russians the monarchy seemed a thing of the past. Nicholas was not a strong ruler as his father had been, and could not adjust to these rapid changes.

When war came to Russia—in 1904–1905 with the Russo-Japanese war, and again in 1914–1918 with World War I—the common people of Russia had to endure starvation, fuel shortages, and catastrophic loss of life in battle, while the rich (including the tsar and his family) seemed almost untouched by these tragedies. During both wars, revolutions erupted in Russia, including workers' strikes, disruption of train service, and violence.

In 1905, Father Georgii Gapon led a peaceful march to the Winter Palace, to appeal to the tsar for help for the starving workers of Russia, and present him with a petition. The tsar's military commanders ordered the soldiers to fire upon the crowd of peaceful demonstrators. Between one hundred fifty and two hundred Russian people were massacred, and hundreds more wounded, in this tragic event that came to be known as "Bloody Sunday," and Nicholas was thereafter known as "Bloody Nicholas." He did not order the murder of Father Gapon's demonstrators. But the night before the march,

Nicholas, who was at Tsarskoye Selo at the time, was told about the planned demonstration and the military's preparations to block it. He chose to remain away from St. Petersburg on the day of the demonstration, and he did nothing to prevent his military and police from using whatever force they thought necessary against the marchers. Nicholas was genuinely horrified by the bloodshed that resulted ("Lord, how painful and sad this is!" he wrote in his diary)—but it was too late. The people rose up in anger against their tsar.

In hopes of stopping the revolution, Tsar Nicholas reluctantly agreed to establish an elected legislature called the Duma (similar to the British parliament). Although some strikes and unrest continued, this seemed to satisfy the people for a while. The war with Japan ended in a defeat for Russia, and Prime Minister Stolypin instituted some reforms that would enable more peasants to own the land that they worked on. During the first revolution, in 1905, the army stayed loyal to the tsar, the unpopular war with Japan ended, and the revolutionaries were disorganized—so the Russian people were ultimately not successful in overthrowing the imperial government. And things calmed down for a while.

However, the Russian royal family remained fearful of assassination attempts in the wake of the 1905 revolution. So after the murder of his Uncle Serge (husband to Alix's sister, Ella), Nicky and his family spent more and more of their time in the relative safety of the Alexander Palace at Tsarskoye Selo, about fifteen miles from the Winter Palace in St. Petersburg. They lived there as a close and happy family, their contentment marred only by the bleeding episodes of young Alexei, who was carried by his sailor-nannies, Nagorny and Derevenko, whenever he was unable to walk. When the boy was well, he was tutored by Pierre Gilliard,‡ Sydney Gibbes, and Peter Petrov.

‡ Gilliard, who was Swiss, survived the Russian Revolution and wrote a sympathetic book about his experiences with Alexei and his family, Thirteen Years at the Russian Court. He died in 1962.

The royal family rarely went out in public, and seemed not to understand the deep discontent growing among their people. When World War I came, costing many

Russian lives, the people were loyal to the tsar at first, but eventually as things got worse and the war dragged on, they could no longer endure the hardships they suffered, and they rose up in revolution. During the February Revolution (1917) a provisional government took over Russia in a coup, and forced Nicholas to abdicate his throne. At first he abdicated in favor of Alexei, but when the doctor explained to him that his hemophiliac son would not be likely to live a normal life span, Nicky abdicated in favor of his brother Michael. ("We bequeath Our inheritance to Our brother the Grand Duke Mikhail Alexandrovich and give him Our Blessing on his accession to the throne.") Under pressure from the revolutionaries to step aside, Michael signed a manifesto agreeing to accept the throne "only if such is the will of our great people, who must now by universal suffrage and through their representatives in the Constituent Assembly establish a form of government and new fundamental laws of the Russian State." But no such vote happened, and some historians say that if one can claim that Michael ever became tsar at all, it was only for a single day. The provisional government, led by Alexander Kerensky, remained in charge.

Nicky's family was kept under house arrest at Tsarskoye Selo from March 1917 until August 1917. After that, the family was moved to Tobolsk, Siberia—supposedly for their own safety, since the provisional government was now being challenged by the Bolsheviks (communists) led by Vladimir Lenin. The Bolsheviks took power in a coup that began in October 1917 and came to be known as the October Revolution. Their harsh Cheka (or All-Russian Extraordinary Commission for Combatting Counter-Revolution and Sabotage)—the Bolsheviks' secret police—helped the Bolsheviks keep control of the new government. But the Bolsheviks were never in a clear majority, and they had many enemies.

After the Bolsheviks signed a peace treaty with Germany (Treaty of Brest-Litovsk in early 1918), which angered many Russians who felt their leaders had "sold out" to an imperialist enemy, the Bolsheviks' power in Russia was challenged again in a civil war. Using Trotsky's tough and well-organized Red Army, the Bolsheviks struggled to keep control of the government—but they were opposed by a number of forces. Most important among these were the government and armies led at first by the Socialist Revolutionaries (moderate socialists), and then the White armies and governments led by Imperial military officers and nobles. All these groups and others tried to force the Bolsheviks out of power. None wanted a return of tsarism, but they also did not want the kind of communist government that the Bolsheviks wanted for Russia.

Forty thousand Czech POWs also were fighting against the Red Army. For a while there were dozens of different types of governments in power in different parts of the Russian empire, and it was unclear who would ultimately win.

Eventually, by the end of 1921, the civil war was over, and the Bolsheviks were firmly in power. They remained so—as the Union of Soviet Socialist Republics—until the Russian Revolution of 1991 that toppled the communists.

One of the causes of the Russian Revolution of 1917–1918 was public outrage against Grigory Efimovich Rasputin—an illiterate self-proclaimed holy man or "starets" (religious advisor or pilgrim; he was not really a priest) born in Siberia in 1872 who gained the complete trust of Tsarina Alexandra. Grigory Efimovich came to be known as "Rasputin," which may derive from the Slavic name "Rasputa" or the word "Raputko," meaning "ill-behaved child." Most language experts say that "Rasputin" comes from the same root as "rasputnik" (libertine) or "rasputstvo," the Russian word for dissipation or debauchery. Others dispute that "Rasputin" had any negative meaning. But, during his lifetime, Rasputin's enemies sometimes also referred to him, contemptuously, as "Grishka."‡ He eventually tried (unsuccessfully) to change his last name to Novy ("newcomer").

‡ "Grishka" is a diminutive for "Grigory," and means something like "little Grigory." So calling the adult Rasputin "Grishka" would be treating him like a child or servant: in other words, as a social inferior.

Rasputin seemed to have the mysterious ability to temporarily stop the bleeding of the hemophiliac heir to the Russian throne, Tsarevich Alexei. Some people today think it's possible that Rasputin hypnotized Alexei, which reduced the boy's stress and helped him recover from his hemophilia attacks. Others say it might have been the power of prayer. But even today, how Rasputin was able to help the boy remains a mystery.

Historian Alex De Jonge writes in his book *The Life And Times of Grigorii Rasputin* that the Mad Monk made "a powerful impression" on those who met him. His eyes "seemed to read their very souls" and "it was claimed by some that he was able to make his pupils expand and contract at will. The voice was strange too. He talked in a thick, almost incomprehensible Siberian accent. . . . His conversation was desperately hard to follow, for he often spoke in riddles . . ."

‡ *A* New York Times *article from November 1912 reported:* Czar's Heir Has Bleeding Disease, *claiming the Russians "announced" this. But Pulitzer Prize–winning Russia historian Robert Massie contends (in his classic book,* Nicholas and Alexandra*) that Alexei's parents had always wanted the boy's illness kept secret and, despite rumors the heir was ill, during Alexei's lifetime ". . . Russia did not know. Most people in Moscow or Kiev or St. Petersburg did not know that the tsarevich had hemophilia, and the few who had some inkling had only hazy ideas about the nature of the disease."*

After Rasputin's telegram to the tsarina (mentioned in this book) seemed to miraculously save Alexei's life during his severe bleeding crisis at the royal family's Polish hunting lodge at Spala in September 1912, Rasputin's hold over the tsarina became total. Alexei's illness was the greatest secret‡ of the Russian royal family. The government was already unstable, and if news got out that the tsarevich was severely ill, the monarchy would have been in even greater danger of being toppled. The Russian people heard rumors the boy was ill, but did not know the precise nature of his illness, nor how severe it really was. They did not understand why weird Rasputin, who had a very bad reputation for drinking and womanizing, and who influenced Russian politics through his close relationship with the tsar and tsarina, was allowed so much control over Russia and the royal family, and why the family listened to his political advice.

Nicky was frequently away at military headquarters in Mogilev during World War I, so Rasputin's influence over the tsarina, and the Russian political decisions made in the tsar's absence, grew even greater.

STATON RABIN

Tsar Nicholas and the tsarina were warned about Rasputin many times, but Alix had total faith in the starets and would not listen to anything bad said about "Our Friend." The tsar went along with her wishes, since he feared that if he banished Rasputin from the palace forever, and Alexei became ill, his son might die and Alix might blame him for the boy's death. But the tsar did send Rasputin away from time to time. And Rasputin's visits to the royal couple and Alexei were kept secret. He would pretend to be visiting one of the servants so that he would not have to sign the royal register that would show that he had actually visited the tsar and tsarina.

There were rumors that Tsarina Alexandra was having a romance with Rasputin. Their relationship was a very close one; she believed that only he had the power to keep her son alive, and the empress's letters to Rasputin—secretly leaked to the press at the time by some of Rasputin's many enemies—are filled with expressions of love. One telegram from the tsarina to Rasputin said: "I sacrifice my husband and my heart to you. Pray and bless. Love and kisses—darling." But it's easy to read too much into this. These letters may just be innocent expressions of affection and deep gratitude, written in the "flowery" style common in the early 1900s. Respected Russian historian Edvard Radzinsky believes there's strong evidence that the empress and Rasputin may have had an affair. But Alix loved her husband Nicky very much, and, judging by the excerpts I've read from their letters to each other and their diaries, I share the opinion of most Romanov scholars that she wasn't unfaithful to him.

Rasputin did not meet the Romanovs till around 1905—when Alexei was about a year old—so even if he and the tsarina were lovers, it's not possible that Rasputin was Alexei's father.

Rasputin was murdered by Felix Yusupov and his coconspirators on the night of December 16–17, 1916. Alexei was not present for Rasputin's murder, and there's no evidence that Alexei suggested that his cousin murder Rasputin.‡ But the

‡ Felix Yusupov and his coconspirators were convinced that the only way to save Russia's monarchy was to get the disreputable Rasputin out of the way. This is why they plotted to murder him—though some historians say that Felix also had a personal vendetta against Rasputin.

remarkable circumstances surrounding Grigory Efimovich's death, as I've described them in this book, and the repeatedly unsuccessful attempts of Prince Felix and his coconspirators to kill the seemingly indestructible starets that night, are really true. Accounts of the murder vary somewhat depending on which eyewitness is telling the story.

On the night of his death, Rasputin told Felix: "The aristocrats can't get used to the idea that a humble peasant should be welcome at the Imperial Palace. They are consumed with envy and fury. But I'm not afraid of them. They can't do anything to me. I'm protected against ill fortune. There have been several attempts on my life but the Lord has always frustrated these plots. Disaster will come to anyone who lifts a finger against me."

He was, it seems, mostly correct. But, weeks earlier, he had correctly predicted the time of his death—saying that he would die "before January 1."

After Rasputin's murder, Tsar Nicholas banished Felix to one of Yusupov's distant palaces, and Dmitri was also sent into exile. This was considered a mere "slap on the wrist," and some historians believe that although Nicholas sympathized with his wife's distress over Rasputin's death, he was rather relieved that the troublesome Rasputin was finally out of the way.

Not long after the murder, Rasputin's bloated corpse floated up from the Neva River—the assassins had failed to weigh down his body. An autopsy showed water in his lungs. This meant that, remarkably, he was still breathing when his rope-bound body was thrown into the river, even after having been already poisoned, shot, and bludgeoned. The Mad Monk's hands were raised in death, as if he had struggled to free himself from his bonds.

‡ They gave a last-minute reprieve to Leonid ("Leonka") Sednev, the kitchen boy who had followed the Romanovs into exile and had befriended Alexei. Leonid was taken from Ipatiev House (which the worried family almost immediately protested) just hours before the murders and was later released unharmed.

Nicholas II, his immediate family, Dr. Botkin, and several servants, were murdered by the Bolsheviks‡ on the night of July 16–17, 1918, at Ipatiev House ("the House of Special Purpose") in Ekaterinburg, Russia. The murders must have been truly horrific, not only for the victims but for the killers as well. Bullets bounced off of several of the victims' bodies. The stunned firing squad didn't know that Alexei's sisters had—at the instructions of their mother—sewn diamonds into their corsets to protect the Romanov family's jewels from being confiscated by the Bolsheviks, and to perhaps eventually use the gems to buy their freedom. When the royal family and their servants went into that basement at Ipatiev House, they had no idea that they were about to be shot. The bullets ricocheted off of the hidden diamonds, and it must have seemed to the assassins that the girls were being protected by some miraculous power. Many of the victims that night died a slow and agonizing death. Yurovsky's men ordered that the girls who survived the fusillade of bullets should be bayoneted until they were dead. Most accounts of the murders say that the tsar and tsarina died instantly from gunshot wounds, but that Alexei had to be finished off with a bullet directly to the head. So much shooting was done in that small room that an hour later, heavy smoke still hung in the air.

It is as hard for me to write about this horrible and tragic event as it may be for some of you to read about it. Perhaps this is why in my own telling of this story, I prefer to imagine that Alexei might have miraculously survived the assassination of the Romanovs by the Bolsheviks that night. Although some have speculated that this might in fact be true, I confess that I believe it is probably just wishful thinking.

For a long time people wondered whether Anastasia or Alexei might have survived the assassination. Given the confusion and secrecy surrounding the assassination of the Romanovs, and the tragedy of their deaths, it is not surprising that many impostors have stepped forward over the years, claiming to be one of the tsar's children. The most famous of these was Anna Anderson, who surfaced back in the 1920s and claimed to be Alexei's sister Anastasia, before DNA testing existed and could have established whether this was true or not. DNA testing long after her death proved beyond doubt that she was not Grand Duchess Anastasia Nicholaevna Romanov.

Another impostor, Vasily Filatov, claimed to be Alexei.

Naturally, any person making such a claim would have to be a hemophiliac. It was never established whether Filatov had hemophilia, nor whether his DNA matched that of the Romanov family. A book, translated into English from Russian, was written about Filatov: *The Escape of Alexei, Son of Tsar Nicholas II* (by multiple authors, published by Harry N. Abrams). Filatov died in 1988.

Most historians believe it's not possible that anyone—least of all Alexei, a hemophiliac—could have survived the barrage of bullets at Ipatiev House that night in 1918.

Decades went by after the murders, and nobody seemed to know for sure where the Romanovs and those murdered with them had been buried. Some of their bones were finally found by self-appointed investigators Alexander Avdonin and Geli Ryabov in 1979 in the Koptyaki Forest. However, the Bolsheviks (now known as the Communists or Soviets) were still in power in Russia at the time. So the two men kept their discovery a secret, reburied the bones, and waited for a change in government.

After the Russian Revolution of 1991 and a change to a more democratic form of government, in the summer of that year Avdonin and Russian archeologists, forensic experts, government officials, and others returned to the grave site to dig up the bones. The bones were later positively identified‡ through DNA testing (comparing "fingerprints" of the DNA in those bones to the DNA patterns of living Romanov relatives and relatives of others killed that night), in the 1990s. For a very detailed account of how the Romanovs' bones were found and identified, read *The Fate of the Romanovs* by Greg King and Penny Wilson (John Wiley & Sons, 2003).

‡ *Although most scientists and historians familiar with the evidence accept the conclusion that these are the bones of the Romanovs, the subject remains controversial. As Harvard professor and Russia historian Donald Ostrowski says, "The case is by no means closed."*

After many delays due to political and religious controversies, on July 17, 1998, the eightieth anniversary of the assassination of the Romanovs, the family's remains received a formal Christian burial at the cathedral of Saint Peter and Saint Paul in St. Petersburg. (The family was also canonized as Christian martyrs, a form of sainthood, by a vote of Russian Orthodox bishops in August 2000.) The burial ceremony was attended by Russian President Boris Yeltsin, Romanov relatives, and others. Saints Peter and Paul is the same cathedral where, traditionally, Russia's Romanov tsars and tsarinas had always been buried. Although nine sets of bones identified as belonging to people assassinated at Ipatiev House on that terrible night in July 1918 have been found, two sets of bones are still missing: those of one of the grand duchesses—either Anastasia or Marie . . .

. . . and the bones of Alexei Romanov.

Russian transliterations: The Russian Cyrillic alphabet is different from the alphabet used in English. In recent decades, Russian words or names have usually been transliterated into English by following the "Library of Congress System"—but there are other acceptable spelling variations, as well. For the Russian words in my book, I've chosen the most simple, easy-to-read English transliterations used by Romanov historians, rather than strictly adhering to the Library of Congress System.

Alexei and each member of his immediate family kept diaries from the time they were children. Occasionally the tsarina would write comments in the tsar's diary—as when she expressed her love for him, shortly after their marriage.

Even decades after the Russian royal family was kidnapped from their home in Tsarskoye Selo, some of the rooms they'd lived in still smelled of rose oil from their icon lamps.

Although Alexei refers to heaven or hell several times in *The Curse of the Romanovs*, and Russian Orthodox Christians do believe in this concept, they think hell and heaven are experiences rather than physical places.

Vaslav Nijinsky (a Pole born in Kiev, Ukraine, circa 1890) studied ballet at Russia's Imperial Theatrical School and upon his graduation in 1907 joined the Mariinsky Theatre's Imperial Ballet. He is considered one of the greatest ballet dancer-choreographers of all time and has been called "the god of dance." Nijinsky worked with and had a personal relationship with legendary ballet impressario Sergei Diaghilev, who collaborated with the choreographer Michel Fokine. One of the ballets that Nijinsky danced in was Stravinsky's *The Rite of Spring*. The music had such a daring, new, modern style that the audience rioted at the first performance in Paris in 1913. Diaghilev's company, the Ballets Russes, starring Nijinsky, was based in Paris. The first ballet that Nijinsky choreographed himself was Debussy's *L'après-midi d'un Faune* ("The Afternoon of a Faun"), which caused another scandal (due to his choreography, not the music).

In 1911 Nijinsky quit the Mariinsky Theatre after an argument over a revealing costume. So, in reality, Nijinsky would not have been in St. Petersburg at the time that Alexei sees him in my book. Nijinsky danced with Diaghilev's Ballets Russes in Paris and South America till 1914. Diaghilev, jealous of Nijinsky's marriage to Hungarian ballerina Romola de Pulszky, fired them both from the Ballets Russes when they returned to Europe that year.

After World War I broke out, the great dancer was held as a prisoner of war in Budapest, Hungary. Nijinsky was released in 1916, when he went on an American tour, reunited with Diaghilev's Ballets Russes. Nijinsky soon began to show signs of insanity: His fellow dancers noticed that he was afraid of them, and that he was worried that he would fall through a trap door on the stage. His illness was diagnosed as schizophrenia, and his career ended with a nervous breakdown in 1919. Nijinsky was in a mental institution in Switzerland from 1932 to 1933, and after 1919 spent most of his life in and out of asylums, during which time he wrote a diary (later published) in two volumes. Nijinsky died in London in 1950.

The husband of the great French writer Colette saw Nijinsky dance at the height of his powers and wrote of him: "Yesterday when Nijinsky took off so slowly and elegantly, describing a trajectory of 4½ meters and landing noiselessly in the wings, an incredulous 'Ah!' burst from the ladies. . . . Since the Romantic period it had been the women, the Muse, the diva, the ballerina who had been worshipped: to admire a man for his grace and beauty was unheard-of."

For more information about Nijinsky, go to:
http://www.nypl.org/research/lpa/nijinsky/home.html
or http://members.tripod.com/Barry_Stone/nijinsky.htm
The Mariinsky Theatre is still open in St. Petersburg, Russia.

HISTORICAL NOTES
(WHAT'S TRUE, WHAT'S NOT)

The Curse of the Romanovs reflects young Alexei Romanov's limited perspective on his parents as rulers, and shows his love and loyalty toward them. This book is by no means intended to be an objective interpretation of Nicholas II's and Empress Alexandra's roles in Russian history. It is clear that Alexei had a loving and well-intentioned family, but it is equally true that his parents' actions (and, in some cases, failure to take action) as rulers resulted in much death and misery in Russia. *The Curse of the Romanovs* is a novel, imagined from Alexei's point of view; for a different and more objective perspective on the Romanovs and the Russian Revolution, you must read history books.

Varda Rosenberg and her family are purely my invention. All the other major characters in *The Curse of the Romanovs* are based on real people.

One of Alexei Romanov's *diadkas* (sailor-nannies), Derevenko—unrelated to his doctor, Derevenko—did in fact turn against the Romanov family after the February Revolution. He angrily ordered Alexei around after the provisional government took power, when the Romanov family was under house arrest. Derevenko was clearly resentful at having once been their servant. However, after he fled the palace, it's not known what happened to him. There's no evidence that Derevenko joined the Red Army.

Nagorny, Alexei's other *diadka*, remained loyally devoted to him and his family till the end. He was with the Romanovs even when they were held captive at Ipatiev House, but was eventually taken away by the Bolsheviks, was jailed in Ekaterinburg, and—unbeknownst to Alexei and his family—was shot and killed just a few days later.

Alexei's nosebleed that started at Mogilev happened in December 1915, not December 1916. I moved it a year ahead to expedite the story and put it closer to the time of Rasputin's murder.

Alexei did indeed speak Russian, English, and French.

Alexei's German-born mother spoke to the children in English, to the servants in Russian, and to her court in French. Tsar Nicholas II spoke Russian to their children, but the letters Alexei's parents exchanged were in English.

The Alexander Palace at Tsarskoye Selo, in which Alexei had lived most of his life, was turned into a museum soon after the Bolsheviks took over Russia. As early as June 23, 1918, the front halls of the former palace were opened to the public for viewing, quickly followed by his parents' personal rooms. Orphans were moved into the royal children's former quarters.

Queen Victoria's daughter Beatrice was indeed Alexei's great-aunt on his mother's side, and she was also a carrier of hemophilia. But the Russian-Jewish painter with whom she had a "forbidden romance" is purely my invention, so that there would be a reasonable explanation for how Varda, a Jewish girl, could be related to Alexei's Russian Orthodox family. There were in fact rumors in Alexei's family that one of his Russian Orthodox uncles, a grand duke, had an affair with a Jewish woman, so royal affairs across boundaries of social class, religion, or ethnicity did sometimes happen during this time.

Before his marriage to Alix, the future Nicholas II did indeed have a lengthy affair with a ballerina, Mathilde Kschessinska, as Alexei's sister mentions in my book. Mathilde later wrote a book about her romance with Nicky and its sad ending. She died in 1971.

St. Petersburg is considered one of the world's most beautiful cities ("The Venice of the North") and is home to over five million people. Of all the world's cities that have a population of over one million, it is the farthest north. The famous "White Nights" of St. Petersburg, during which the sun never sets, normally last from June eleventh to July second each year. In my story I continued this period to July tenth, so that Alexei and Varda could experience the Beliye Noche.

In real life, Rasputin did not survive Felix's final attempt to kill him by tossing him into the Neva. He died in December 1916. And of course Alexei Romanov did not travel to the future between then and July 1918, when his family was murdered. He was with his family the entire time they were in exile following Tsar Nicholas's abdication—except during a few weeks in the spring of 1918, when Alexei and three of his sisters remained captive at Tobolsk while his parents and Grand Duchess Marie were sent on to their final imprisonment at Ipatiev House in the Ural Mountains.

What caused this temporary family separation? Alexei was too ill to travel. He had injured himself sledding down the stairs inside the house at Tobolsk. This started internal bleeding that threatened his life. Nicky said that it was as if Alexei had hurt himself on purpose. During the worst of this crisis, Alexei told the tsarina, "Mama, I would like to die. I am not afraid of death, but I am so afraid of what they will do to us here."

The family's captors insisted that the tsar must be moved to another location immediately. The tsarina had a terrible decision to make. Did she stay with her ailing son, or go on to Ekaterinburg with her husband? She agonized over the problem.

At last Alix made her decision: "You know what my son is to me," she said to her staff, "and I must choose between him and my husband. But I have made up my mind. I must be firm. I must leave my child and share my husband's life or death."

The family was reunited at Ipatiev House in late May 1918, and remained together until their deaths. It is for me at least some consolation to know that this very close and loving family was together during their final moments.

In the spring and summer of 1918, at seven o'clock every morning, Sisters Antonina and Maria of the Novotikhvinsky Convent in Ekaterinburg were permitted to bring extra food in baskets to Ipatiev House for the imprisoned Romanovs, right up until the day of the royal family's murder.

Tsar Nicholas II did read Sir Arthur Conan Doyle's Sherlock Holmes stories to Alexei and the rest of his family, so it is likely that Alexei was familiar with the first short story featuring the Great Detective, "A Scandal in Bohemia," which describes Holmes's and Watson's use of a "smoke-rocket."

Ipatiev House did have a parlor downstairs, but for my story I placed the only couch on the upper floor, so that Alexei could be sure that Varda would be brought there after "fainting." Only the attic windows of the house would have been fully visible from the street, over the top of the high wooden fence surrounding it. Even though some of the guards got drunk at times, the house was so well guarded—especially after Yurovksy took over as commandant—that no intruder would have been able to get as close to it as Alexei did.

Some of Ipatiev House's windows were whitewashed so that the family couldn't see outside their quarters except through a very small upper unpainted portion of one window. The windows on the upper floor were only rarely opened while the Romanovs were held captive there, so the summer heat inside could be stifling. At least one window had metal bars placed over it, at Yurovsky's orders. Prior to this, the tsarina used to wave a handkerchief out the window, hoping to be seen by passersby on the street.

There were originally ten guard posts inside and outside the house. But when Yurovsky took over as commandant, he added two more guard posts, because he was worried that somebody might try to rescue the family. He also believed that several of the guards were becoming too friendly with the Romanovs—and some of Alexei's sisters, especially Marie, had been flirting with the guards. So Yurovksy fired and replaced some of the guards, and moved others to posts farther away from the family's section of the house. Still, he had difficulty finding enough men willing to shoot the family. Several were especially reluctant to kill Alexei's sisters. And, after the murder, some who participated in the firing squad or who had guarded the family before their deaths seemed to feel guilty and tormented about what they had done.

Coincidentally, at least one of the guards at the House of Special Purpose, Kabanov, had known Alexei's family before the tsar abdicated. Olga recognized the man as one of their former grenadier guards, and reintroduced him to the tsar, who also remembered having met him before.

Alexei was not able to walk in the final few days of his life. On July 13 he bumped himself in the bathtub at Ipatiev House.

A few days later his father carried the pale and sickly boy into the room in which the family was to meet their tragic fate.

The Bolsheviks were slow to admit that the royal family had been murdered. Even when they announced to the public on July 20 that the tsar had been killed, they falsely claimed that Alexei, his mother, and his sisters were alive and had been taken to a safe location.

Alexei's tutor Pierre Gilliard had bravely chosen to stay with him while the boy and his family were being held captive by the Bolsheviks. Although Gilliard traveled with Alexei when the Romanovs were moved from Tsarskoye Selo to Tobolsk and from there to Ipatiev House, the Bolsheviks separated Gilliard from Alexei on May 22.

For reasons that even Gilliard himself didn't understand, the Bolsheviks spared the tutor's life and set him free. He caught a quick glimpse of Alexei on May 23, when Nagorny carried the ailing boy past Gilliard's train car window at Ekaterinburg. But after that, Gilliard never saw Alexei and his family again. In my story, I chose to keep Gilliard with the Romanov family till the last full day of their lives, so that Alexei could have a chance to say the final good-bye to him that he never got in real life.

Just days after the murders, with Ekaterinburg now in the White Army's hands, Gilliard and Alexei's English tutor, Mr. Gibbes, returned to Ipatiev House on a desperate search for the boy and his family. They even inspected the room in which the family had been killed, still hoping against hope that perhaps somehow the children might have escaped the horrific bloody murder scene. But within months, traces of the Romanov family's bodies and belongings were found in the nearby forest, and it was clear that all hope for their survival was lost.

Alexei and his immediate family were not the only Romanovs killed by the Bolsheviks in this era. Among the dozens of other family members killed were Alexei's uncle Misha (Nicholas II's younger brother Michael Romanov, who, briefly, was his designated replacement as tsar after Nicholas abdicated), and Alexei's aunt Ella, his mother's sister.

Starting on February 1, 1918, the Russian system of keeping track of days and months changed from the Julian calendar to the Gregorian calendar—a difference of thirteen days. The Russians were in fact behind most of the rest of the world in adopting the modern, Gregorian calendar, which is still used today. Alexei was born on July 30 under the Julian calendar ("old style") and on August 12 according to the Gregorian system ("new style"). Beginning in 1918 the tsar and tsarina used two dates for each day listed in their diaries, representing the old and new systems. Some modern books about Russian history don't say whether they are using dates from the Julian or Gregorian calendar. To avoid confusion on this issue in my own book, I identify pre-1918 events by their month, season, or year rather than their precise day, so that the dates would be correct regardless of whether one uses the old or new calendar system. Dates for events from early 1918 on follow the modern (Gregorian) calendar.‡

‡ The one exception is Alexei's fourteenth birthday, which, in my story, the tsarevich believes will take place on July 30, 1918, because from his perspective the Julian calendar was never replaced.

To compress time, I combined into a single meeting on July 13 several key meetings of the Ural Soviet and the Cheka that took place in late June and early July 1918 in room number 3 at the Hotel Amerika in Ekaterinburg. During these meetings the presidium replaced Avdeyev with Yurovsky as commandant of Ipatiev House (July 3), and passed a resolution to murder the Romanovs (June 29). Their resolution calling for the liquidation of Nicholas II and his family required that the family be killed no later than July 15, 1918—which the Ural Soviet believed was the last possible date before the Czech and White armies would invade Ekaterinburg. In my story, to avoid confusing the reader, I moved this target date forward by twenty-four hours, to the actual day that the Romanovs were murdered: the night of July 16–17, 1918. The counterrevolutionary forces that might have rescued Alexei and his family took over Ekaterinburg on July 25, just eight days after they were killed.

Alexei's parents, Nicky and Alix (Tsar Nicholas II and Tsarina Alexandra), were cousins. Here's how they were related:

Nicky's aunt, Alexandra of Denmark, had married Edward VII, the son of Queen Victoria of England. So from then on, Nicky was related by marriage to the British royal family. When Nicky married Alix, he was marrying a granddaughter of Queen Victoria who was also Edward VII's niece. Alix's mother was Princess Alice, one of Queen Victoria's daughters.

However, Princess Alice died when her daughter Alix was only six years old. After Princess Alice died, Queen Victoria of England took a personal interest in raising her granddaughter, Alix. This is why Alexei's mother spoke English fairly well, adopted many English customs, and considered herself more British than German. When she married the future Tsar Nicholas II, she considered herself Russian as well.

Hemophilia is inherited in families through females. Alexei's grandmother Princess Alice inherited the defective gene that causes the disease from her mother, Queen Victoria. Princess Alice passed it down to her daughter Alix—who in turn "gave" it to her son, Alexei Romanov. Alix's sister Irene passed the disease into another royal family when she married and had children with Prince Henry of Prussia.

Since Alexei's father Nicholas II was related to Queen Victoria only by marriage, his side of the family did not carry the disease of hemophilia.

Alexei's mother and father knew that there was hemophilia in the tsarina's family. In addition to Alix's mother, Princess Alice, two of Queen Victoria's other daughters, Princesses Beatrice and Victoria, were also carriers of the disease, and one of her sons, Leopold, had hemophilia. Alix's brother, Frittie, died at age three due to excessive bleeding following a fall.

It will never be known whether Alexei's sisters, Olga, Tatiana, Marie, and Anastasia, might have been carriers of hemophilia. They died before having any children, and in those days there were no blood or genetic tests to determine whether a female was a "silent" carrier of the disease. But since their mother Tsarina Alexandra was a carrier, the odds are that about half of Alexei's sisters were also carriers of hemophilia.

When Nicky's and Alix's family were murdered, this ended not only the Russian monarchy but also the further transmission of the "hemophilia gene" on that branch of the family tree—which *might* have occurred had their children lived to have children of their own.

The current Queen of England, Elizabeth II, and her husband Prince Philip are related to Queen Victoria and the Romanovs. However, through a stroke of good fortune, the British royal couple's branches of the family tree were spared from this terrible disease, because their more recent ancestors did not carry it. Queen Elizabeth II is descended from Queen Victoria's son Edward VII, who did not have hemophilia.

When scientists today do DNA tests to determine whether certain individuals or their bones might really be from the Romanov family, they sometimes compare these DNA patterns to DNA samples taken from England's Prince Philip, who is a blood relative of Alexei's mother, Tsarina Alexandra, and has cooperated in these experiments.

Facts About Hemophilia

There is currently no cure for hemophilia, which affects about 18,000 people in the United States‡ and is just one of a number of diseases that can reduce the clotting of the blood. The disease is much more common in boys, since (as Varda explains in *The Curse of the Romanovs*) a girl would usually have to inherit the defective gene from both parents in order to have symptoms of hemophilia. Females, however, are the "silent" carriers of the disease, and sometimes even carriers can need treatment for excessive bleeding.

‡ *and many others, of course, around the globe. About 1 in 5,000 males is born with hemophilia.*

Although hemophilia is mainly an inherited illness, 30 percent of hemophiliacs have no known family history of the disease.

Males who inherit hemophilia had a mother who carried the defective gene, since this gene is never carried on the Y chromosome that boys inherit from their fathers. This means that, paradoxically, the son of a hemophiliac can never be a hemophiliac—unless the boy's mother *also* carries the disease (or unless the son was born with hemophilia purely by coincidence, through a spontaneous gene mutation)! However, all the daughters of a hemophiliac male will be carriers of the illness, since his only X chromosome has the defective gene.

Hemophilia not only results in excessive bleeding when the hemophiliac is injured, but may sometimes even cause dangerous episodes of spontaneous bleeding—in the brain, for example—without any obvious cause. Repeated or severe episodes of bleeding can cause permanent damage to joints, vision loss, chronic anemia, neurological or psychiatric problems, and, of course, death.

Contrary to popular belief, a superficial cut is not dangerous to a hemophiliac—applying pressure to the injury can stop the bleeding. But bumps or spontaneous internal bleeding are far more serious, since they can cause a buildup of pressure in a confined space.

People today who have hemophilia are mainly treated with infusions of genetically engineered blood clotting factors, factor

VIII and factor IX‡ to prevent or control excessive bleeding. Hemophiliacs are often taught how to give themselves this treatment at home, but sometimes it must be done by medical staff at hospitals or treatment centers. There are several different types of hemophilia, and Alexei probably had the most common type, known today as hemophilia A (but Alexei's exact diagnosis is, like almost everything else about the Romanovs, a hot topic of debate).

‡ *Those with mild cases of the disease might be treated with the synthetic hormone DDAVP, which stimulates the body's own production of factor VIII.*

Some people have milder forms of hemophilia without even being aware of it; their illness may become noticeable only if they bleed excessively during major surgery.

Gene therapy may soon offer hope in curing this terrible illness. If this treatment succeeds in raising levels of clotting factors in the blood of hemophiliacs by even only 2 percent, this will be enough to prevent spontaneous bleeding episodes in organs and joints, which can kill. Since hemophilia is the result of a defect on only one gene, scientists consider it a promising candidate for potential treatment through gene therapy.

You can find out more information about hemophilia, or donate money toward finding a cure, by contacting the National Hemophilia Foundation at www.hemophilia.org.

PARTIAL LIST OF SOURCES FOR *THE CURSE OF THE ROMANOVS*:

The Russian Revolution, 1917, Rex A. Wade. Cambridge University Press. 2005.

Thirteen Years at the Russian Court, Pierre Gilliard. Trans. by F. Appleby Holt. London: Hutchinson & Co. 1921.

The Flight of the Romanovs, John Curtis Perry and Constantine Pleshakov. New York: Basic Books. 1999.

The Last Tsar: The Life and Death of Nicholas II, Edvard Radzinsky. Trans. by Marian Schwartz. New York: Doubleday. 1992.

The Fate of the Romanovs, Greg King and Penny Wilson. Hoboken, NJ: John Wiley & Sons. 2003.

Tsar: The Lost World of Nicholas and Alexandra, Peter Kurth. Boston: Little, Brown. 1995.

The Russian Revolution, Richard Pipes. New York: Knopf. 1990.

Sunlight at Midnight: St. Petersburg and the Rise of Modern Russia, W. Bruce Lincoln. Boulder, Colo: Basic Books. 2000.

The Rasputin File, Edvard Radzinsky. Trans. by Judson Rosengrant. New York: Nan A. Talese. 2000.

The Life and Times of Grigorii Rasputin, Alex De Jonge. New York: Coward, McCann, and Geoghegan. 1982. (Reprinted Barnes & Noble Books, 1993.)

Nicholas and Alexandra, Robert K. Massie. New York: Atheneum. 1967.

The Romanovs: The Final Chapter, Robert K. Massie. New York: Random House. 1995.

Nicholas II: The Imperial Family, Abris Publications,
    St. Petersburg, Peterhof. 2002.

Left Behind: Fourteen Months in Siberia During the Revolution,
    December 1917–February 1919, by Baroness Sophie
    Buxhoeveden (lady-in-waiting to Empress Alexandra
    Feodorovna of Russia).

Alexander II: The Last Great Tsar, Edvard Radzinsky. Trans. by
    Antonina W. Bouis. New York: Free Press. 2005.

"The Alexander Palace of Tsarskoye Selo After the Romanovs,"
    lecture by Iraida Bott and Larisa Bardovskaya. The State
    Museum (Tsarskoye Selo), St. Petersburg. Access to paper
    courtesy of Ms. Bott, and Una Belau of Yale University's
    Beinecke Rare Book and Manuscript Library, 2004.

There are a great many websites about Alexei Romanov,
Rasputin, and the Russian royal family, where members and
visitors can study these subjects—and debate issues such as
whether Alexei or any members of his immediate family could
have survived the assassination.

Some websites of interest include:

The Alexander Palace Time Machine
http://www.alexanderpalace.org/palace/
This beautifully designed Web site also has a discussion forum.

Alexei's Hemophilia: The Triangle Affair of Nicholas II,
Alexandra, and Rasputin
http://it.stlawu.edu/~rkreuzer/pcaron/alexisillness.html

The First Alexei Nicholaevich Romanov Web Page
http://members.aol.com/Dangit0/Alexei/main.htm

Alexei Romanov Page
http://www.geocities.com/Vienna/9463/alexei.html